A Wedding

You are cordially invited to the wedding of the century...

Heiress Ivy Jenkins and CEO Sebastian Davis— Manhattan's It Couple!—are set to tie the knot at New York's *ultimate* wedding venue: Parker & Parker.

With their guest list a who's who of the city's A-Listers, Ivy and Sebastian want a wedding to remember! So they need the best in the business to help plan their perfect day... Cue Alexandra Harris, Hailey Thomas and Autumn Jones! The wedding planner, florist and maid of honor may be there to make Ivy and Sebastian's day magical... but what if their love lives receive a sprinkle of Christmas magic, too?

Discover Alexandra and Drew's story in

The Wedding Planner's Christmas Wish
by Cara Colter

Hailey and Giovanni's story in

Prince's Christmas Baby Surprise
by Ellie Darkins

and

Autumn and Jack's story in

Reunited Under the Mistletoe by Susan Meier

Available now!

Dear Reader,

Welcome to Adria! I'm so excited that you are about to meet its crown prince, Gianna (just Gio to his friends), and the woman who's about to turn his life upside down.

This book was such a joy to write, especially as I got to collaborate with my brilliant colleagues Cara Colter and Susan Meier, both of whom were supremely generous with their time and advice while writing their own gorgeous stories.

Now it's over to you: settle in somewhere cozy, light a candle or two to set the scene and prepare to lose yourself in an (almost!) fairy tale. I can't want to hear what you think of it!

Love,

Ellie Darkins

Prince's Christmas Baby Surprise

Ellie Darkins

Special thanks and acknowledgment are given to Ellie Darkins for her contribution to the A Wedding in New York miniseries.

Recycling programs
for this product may
not exist in your area.

ISBN-13: 978-1-335-40687-3

Prince's Christmas Baby Surprise

Copyright © 2021 by Harlequin Books S.A.

This edition published by arrangement with Harlequin Books S.A.

For questions and comments about the quality of this book, please contact us at CustomerService@Harlequin.com.

Harlequin Enterprises ULC
22 Adelaide St. West, 40th Floor
Toronto, Ontario M5H 4E3, Canada
www.Harlequin.com

Printed in U.S.A.

Ellie Darkins spent her formative years devouring romance novels and, after completing her English degree, decided to make a living from her love of books. As a writer and editor, she finds her work now entails dreaming up romantic proposals, hot dates with alpha males and trips to the past with dashing heroes. When she's not working, she can usually be found running around after her toddler, volunteering at her local library or escaping all the above with a good book and a vanilla latte.

Books by Ellie Darkins

Harlequin Romance

Visit the Author Profile page at Harlequin.com.

For Betty Darkins

1928–2020

Thank you for letting me borrow your books and
your name.

Praise for
Ellie Darkins

"All in all, this is another enjoyable, heartfelt,
emotional romance from Ellie Darkins with
characters you care about, and look forward to
following their journey throughout the book. A
thoroughly enjoyable story...which will leave you
smiling, and perhaps crying a few happy tears
along the way. An excellent read."

—*Goodreads* on *Falling Again for Her Island Fling*

CHAPTER ONE

IF SOMEONE HAD told him that being best man for his old university friend would mean being dragged to a freezing cold floristry studio less than an hour after his plane had touched down in New York, Gio might have reconsidered his answer.

He caught the florist's eye and stifled a yawn as he followed his friend Sebastian, Sebastian's fiancée, Ivy, and their wedding planner, Alexandra, into the freezing cold studio-slash-workshop where they were to inspect the proposed floral displays for the upcoming wedding. He glanced over the arrangements that the florist had laid out for them and had to admit to being slightly impressed. He knew nothing about flowers, but these seemed bold and artistic, and would not have looked out of place alongside the Dutch masters that graced the walls of the palace in Adria. He could tell from their spellbound expressions that Sebastian and Ivy were impressed too, and that was good enough for him.

He watched the florist speaking to Ivy and Sebastian and tried to catch her eye again, but she was focused entirely on his friends, which gave him an opportunity to get a better look without giving himself away. She was cute. Very cute. More than a head shorter than him, with a soft, wavy bob that finished just below her jaw and a fringe that framed her face, highlighting pixie-like features and a delicately pointed chin. There was something about the soft roundness of her petite frame that made him want to pick her up and tuck her into his pocket. And something about the determination in her face as Alexandra quizzed her on the costings and the details of delivery and timings that told him for sure that she'd kick him if he even tried it. Intriguing.

He tried to concentrate on what she was saying, but he knew he was fighting a losing battle with fatigue. He was aware that his shirt was still creased from where it had got crumpled in his bag, and his stubble was about a day and a half beyond actually being stubble. The time difference between New York and Adria meant that he had been awake way into the night, and he'd only had just enough time to throw himself into the shower when Sebastian had hammered on his door a few minutes before they were meant to be leaving for their meetings with various wedding suppliers. Sebastian had insisted that Gio be in on all the details so he could step in if there were any problems on the big day. Not that he could possibly anticipate any, given the fierce efficiency of the wedding planner. But when things went wrong it was altogether unsurprising that a crown prince could get results just by asking nicely.

His mother would be horrified if she could see him now, and no doubt would have all sorts of things to say about how, as Crown Prince of Adria, he was representing their tiny nation on the world stage and he should occasionally present himself as if he remembered that fact. It was a shame, really, for all involved, that the more his mother seemed to remind him of things like that, the more he wanted to act like a teenager and ignore her just to make a point.

He hadn't asked to be a crown prince. No one would choose to have their life mapped out from the day they were born: where they would live, what they would do every single day of their lives…who they would marry.

He looked at Ivy and Sebastian, both of them glowing in that wholesome way that they had whenever they were talking about the wedding, which considering it was in just over ten weeks' time was pretty much all they had talked about since he had arrived in the country. And he contrasted that warm glow with the haughty iciness that his parents exuded in their wedding photos—a wedding, and a marriage, that had been planned to suit the families involved rather than the individuals who were taking the vows. An uncomfortable foreshadowing of his own future.

He tried to shake off the feeling of dread, because so far he'd managed to deflect all suggestions from his parents that he really should be married by now. Neither of them was exactly delighted with the shambolic state of their union, after all, and perhaps they had the good sense to try and protect their firstborn from sharing their fate for as long as possible. But he knew that it couldn't last for ever. Eventually, he would have to marry, and he wouldn't be the one choosing the 'lucky' woman. The best that he could hope for was that he didn't entirely hate his partner, the way his parents had come to hate one another.

A shiver passed through him at this portent of his future, and he looked at the florist again. Was she the sort of girl that he would marry if he had the choice? He tried to imagine it. A future where he got to choose what he wanted. *Who* he wanted. And found that he couldn't. He'd spent so long resigned to the fact that he wouldn't get to choose his life partner that he couldn't imagine what he would do with free choice even if he had it.

That shiver of dread had kicked off some sort of chain reaction in his body and, before he even knew what was happening, somehow a yawn was creeping up on him and, although he fought it hard, it escaped him, stretching his jaw out of shape and drawing the attention of everyone in the room.

'Oh, I'm sorry, are we keeping you awake?' the florist asked, and he was torn between amusement at the expression on her face and mortification that he'd just yawned during what could potentially be one of the more important meetings of her life.

'I'm so sorry, Miss...'

'Ms,' she supplied. 'Thomas. Hailey Thomas.'

'I'm so sorry, Ms Thomas,' he started again. 'The blame lies entirely with me and my jet lag and not with your delightful...' He had to think for a moment to find the right word in English, a language he had been speaking every day since he had gone to boarding school in the UK at eleven. It was simply fatigue that had scrambled his thoughts, he told himself. Not the presence of Ms Thomas. 'Creations,' he finished, limply.

'You're a fan of my work?' she asked, her hands planted on her hips and her mouth quirking up at one corner, just enough for him to see that she had a sense of humour, and somehow he was hitting her buttons. Well, that was an interesting development. Because, as he looked her up and down, he was certain that there were a couple of other buttons he wouldn't mind uncovering.

'They're very beautiful,' he said, honestly appraising what he could see of her work. Not that his opinion should count for much—he was hardly an authority here. This was entirely her field, and he wouldn't dream of trying to explain it to her.

'Thank you,' she said, turning back to Ivy, Sebastian and Alexandra to continue their meeting, and he considered himself dismissed. He slunk at the back of the room, his eyes never leaving Ms Thomas as she talked them through various options, pulling flowers out of arrangements and offering them up for Ivy's inspection, occasionally sketching something on her notepad, and listening thoughtfully to the feedback from the couple.

He could just go to bed, he told himself. If he did that, there was a small chance that he would sleep right through to tomorrow morning and wake up feeling human again. Or, on the other hand, he could stay here watching Ms Thomas spilling Latin flower names picturesquely from her lips: a hitherto unknown turn-on. They were wrapping things up, he realised, snapping his mind to attention, and out of the fantasy of Hailey Thomas whispering into his ear.

'Ms Thomas,' he said, rather louder than he'd intended, and the four other people in the room all snapped their heads to look at him.

The woman he'd been addressing merely raised her eyebrows a fraction in response.

'I was wondering if you'd allow me to take you to dinner,' he said, the first idea that popped into his head. 'As an apology for my lapse in manners.'

She stared at him for a moment, her eyes appraising. 'Wouldn't you rather go to bed?' she asked, and for just a moment the room was in perfect silence as they all absorbed what she'd just said, and then all started speaking at once.

'Well, of course I considered that too, but—'

'Gio!' Seb cut in.

'I… I meant…' Hailey stuttered. 'I meant jet lag! Because you *yawned*—'

She stared at him as they all paused in the heavy, uncomfortable atmosphere. 'Thank you, I'd be delighted,' she said at last in a frostily professional voice, and then snapped her notebook closed and turned on her heel to address Ivy, Seb and Alexandra. 'Ms Jenkins, Mr Davis, it's been a pleasure. Please let me know if you have any more questions; otherwise, I'll see you just before the big day.'

She turned, more slowly, to him. 'Mr… I mean, Your Royal…' She trailed off, and he realised they hadn't even been properly introduced.

'Gio,' he said quickly, wanting to slice through the formalities. 'I'm Gio to my friends.'

'Gio, then. I'll meet you in the lobby of your hotel at eight.'

He nodded. 'I'm staying at the Ritz-Carlton.'

And with that Hailey swept from the room and left everyone in it—himself very much included—more than a little in love with her.

If only he had the sort of life where falling just a little bit in love with someone made a blind bit of difference to his future, he might have been a little excited.

CHAPTER TWO

WHAT THE HELL had she just agreed to? And why? Dinner with a prince? In public—because there was no way that she was meeting up with him in private after both of them seemed to have lost their wits in that meeting with Sebastian, Ivy and Alexandra.

This was going to be a nightmare. She had already embarrassed herself spectacularly—there was no good reason to give herself the opportunity to make things worse. Well, she supposed things *couldn't* get much worse than accidentally propositioning him.

She took a moment to wonder how accidental that had actually been. Because, while of course she didn't mean to suggest that they should go to bed together in front of her clients—his friends—she would be lying if the thought hadn't been there in her mind and then just slightly…escaped. She couldn't help but wonder either what exactly his reaction would have been if she *had* propositioned him. If, for the sake of argument, they had been alone in the room and able to explore that idea properly.

She shook her head. That was never going to happen. She wasn't in the habit of going around propositioning princes of tiny European countries she'd barely heard of, and she wasn't going to make a start now. It didn't take a genius to see that that could lead to nothing but complication and heartache. She had had a simple start in life, had already reinvented herself once with her big transatlantic move, and the last thing that her life needed was another sphere where she didn't belong.

But it was one dinner—she was hardly signing herself up for a lifetime of public appearances. All she had to do was eat one meal, accept his apology for yawning—*yawning*—while she was trying to pin down the details of the trim for Ivy's bouquet, and that would be that. She'd never have to see him again, not unless he sought her out to go through the arrangements for the flowers the weekend of the wedding, and she somehow predicted that that wouldn't be high on his list of priorities.

Hailey strode into the hotel lobby at a minute past eight, determined not to be caught fidgeting or awkwardly waiting for Gio. If he wasn't here, she'd simply turn around and walk out again. One chance—that was all he was getting. And half a dozen times in the past few hours she had decided that she wouldn't even give him that. She would have cancelled, had he not been a friend of her clients. This job was the biggest of her career, and she wasn't going to risk upsetting the bride and groom by standing up the best man.

Of course he was there. Because the sight of him unnerved her—and it seemed he could always be counted on to unsettle her as much as possible. He did it on purpose, she was sure. She couldn't explain *why* she was so sure. It was only that…surely no one could have this much of an effect on her by *accident*, simply by existing in proximity to her.

She saw the moment that he spotted her across the room and tried not to read anything into the gleam in his eye. It was just a flicker of light. There was nothing to interpret there. This dinner was just as he had said: a formality to excuse his lapse in manners when he'd yawned during their meeting. He wasn't… interested in her. That much was made clear in the collective mortification and embarrassment in the room following her gaffe about him going to bed.

He was a prince—and she didn't belong in his world any more than he belonged in hers of 4:00 a.m. flower markets, thermal base layers and hands chapped from bleaching buckets in the cold. With Ivy and Sebastian, her place and her role were clear. She was the hired help. And she was comfortable and secure knowing that. But this development was throwing that security on its head and leaving her uncomfortably adrift. She hated that feeling. Had run from it, all the way from West London suburbia to New York.

Because, strangely, so far from home, she knew that she *shouldn't* belong. After a childhood spent moving from family to family, children's home to children's home, she had tried over and over again to feel as if she was a part of something. As if she truly belonged with the family she had been placed with this time. And she'd smiled and tried so hard to be good. It had been exhausting, and it had never worked, so that by the time the revolving door of foster homes had stopped—and she had finally been adopted by a kind, loving couple who had tried everything to make her feel a part of their family—she was beyond it. Perhaps, when her birth parents had given her away, it had severed any chance that she would feel entitled to have a link to any place, any people, that would be hers.

New York had been such a relief. A place where she was declared a misfit by the stamp in her passport. Where she didn't have to try and belong any more. She could just be herself in a city filled with misfits. And so she had relaxed into it. Into her art history studies, for which she had moved halfway across the world. Into her talent for floristry, which she had discovered when a part-time job had overlapped with her art course and created something quite magical. And marketable. And in her boss, Gracie, she had made a dear friend, who felt more like a mother than the circus of people who had played a part in her childhood.

She wouldn't fit into Gio's world, but that didn't matter for the space of a dinner. She'd had plenty of practice not belonging. It was only a night, and she did know how to be a tourist.

'You came,' Gio said, greeting her with a dazzling smile and a kiss to both cheeks.

'I thought that was the general idea,' she said, raising her eyebrows a fraction and stepping half a pace back. Preserving her personal space. Because standing too close to Gio had an effect on her that she didn't want to think too much about. The sort of dizzying, pulse-racing, thought-distracting effect that made it hard to remember not to be swept away by those Mediterranean good looks and impeccable manners, no doubt polished at a finishing school somewhere—or whatever wood-panelled, cigar-smoke-fugged, whisky-soaked men's club princes were sent to, rather than a school that taught young ladies how to get out of cars without flashing their knickers.

At least, that was what she assumed royalty did. Her upbringing hadn't exactly given her a great view of the curriculum of European finishing schools.

'Well, I'm delighted to see you,' he said, smoothing over her prickliness. 'I booked a table at the restaurant here. If that suits.'

Dinner at the Ritz-Carlton, and Prince Charming for company? She supposed it suited.

He offered his arm as a formal invitation to accompany him and she took it, momentarily dizzy at the feeling that she was walking into someone else's life. She shook it off, as she had so many times before.

'Your displays this afternoon were very beautiful,' Gio said as they were seated, and the eye-roll escaped her before she could help it. 'You don't believe me?' he asked, raising an eyebrow, the corner of his mouth turning up in a smile.

'Oh, I think you made your feelings very clear.'

'Ah. The Yawn.'

'The Yawn.' She smiled despite herself, because the abashed look on his face was anything but princely. 'But you gave me the gift of your company by way of apology, so how can I possibly be cross?'

His eyes widened. 'Why is it that every word you speak gives me the impression that you mean the exact opposite?' Gio asked as a waiter arrived with a bottle of champagne that he must have ordered in advance and poured two glasses.

She suppressed a smile because this evening was already proving more enjoyable than she had imagined it might, and the surprise threatened to throw her off-guard. It seemed as if there was a chance that Prince Giovanni of Adria was more than just a pretty face: he could make her laugh too, and wasn't that a dangerous combination...

'Well, if we're not going to discuss your work—'

'And you don't work,' Hailey cut in without thinking, the words slipping from her lips as she concentrated on her menu. She looked up as soon as she realised what she'd said, her lips a small O of surprise.

Gio was grinning at her, and the sight made her stomach flip. He smiled with his whole face. Not just the curl of a lip or a crinkle at the corner of his eyes. She was talking wide smile, dimples, deep crow's feet. *Twinkling* eyes. The whole works. So bright that she suspected that some of it was reflected in her own face.

And she knew she was in so much trouble.

His cheeks hurt. Which was the strangest way to measure the success of a date, but there they were. Three hours into dinner with Hailey Thomas and he had spent every moment of it absolutely delighted. She made him laugh with everything she did. Everything she said. She made him smile most when she was actively trying to annoy him, which had been her default setting for the first half hour or so, until she had seen how much it had amused him and she'd reined in her claws and conceded that she wasn't going to get a rise out of him.

They'd quickly run out of small talk about the wedding and Ivy and Sebastian, and she'd seemed averse to talking about her life. So he'd answered her questions about Adria, told her of its sparkling lakes in the summer and ski resorts in the winter, how they spent early December at the ski lodge in the mountains, before returning to the palace for Christmas. How his father had fought to keep its independence. He'd asked her what he should see while he was in New York, and she'd answered with the names of parks and galleries he'd never heard of.

And the teasing and the eye-rolling and the gentle laughter between them had felt so *easy*, so natural, that he could let himself pretend for a minute. Pretend the fact that he was halfway besotted with Hailey actually mattered outside of this moment. That anyone in the palace, in the entire kingdom of Adria at all, cared about whether this was a good date or a bad date, for that matter.

Any feelings he had for another person would always come second to the demands of his family. His position. His parents would select a bride who would strengthen Adria's place in Europe, and the best that he could hope for was that it wasn't someone he hated on sight. That it wasn't someone he would come to hate. At the very least, he had to hope he would be happier than his parents, who had despised one another for as long as he could remember.

He shook his head—the last thing he should be thinking about was the myriad ways his parents had conspired to make one another miserable. No. Right now he was only interested in Hailey. And—if he was reading this situation right—all the ways they might be able to make each other happy. Just for tonight.

She was here, for a start. Sending him interested, heated glances any time she thought that he wasn't looking. It was amazing, the things she could do to him with just a flicker of her eyes caught in his peripheral vision. He leaned forward, resting his elbows on the edge of the table, trying to follow the movement of her hands as she told him about the first time that she had visited a flower market.

She used at least a dozen words he had never heard before. At least a dozen more in Latin, and he wanted to ask her what each and every one of them meant. Wanted to watch the plump curve of her lips as she explained them to him. He imagined trying to make her come apart as she did so. How he would tease her while she explained the different varieties to him. She would fight hard to keep her head, not to lose control and give in to the pleasure. She'd resist out of principle, wanting to be the one in command, and he would savour every loosening bond until she was incoherent and coming against his mouth.

He realised he had lost the thread of conversation when she cleared her throat.

'Am I boring you?' she asked him, her eyebrows raised in challenge. 'Again?'

'Not at all. I just find myself momentarily distracted.'

'By?' Hailey asked, with an arched eyebrow to accompany that single word that suggested she knew exactly the direction his thoughts had taken.

'By you.'

'Ah.' She stared at him for a moment, seemed to be considering her options. 'What was I doing?' she asked sweetly.

'I don't think it's wise to tell you,' he said honestly, feeling suddenly flushed. Like a schoolboy who'd been caught doing something he shouldn't.

'I think I like distracting you,' Hailey said, sitting back in her chair and taking a sip of wine, fixing him with an assessing glare.

'I think I like it when you look at me like that,' Gio said in a low voice. Her gaze stripped him bare. Bare of his skin, as if she could see every one of his secrets. He had no doubt that he could keep nothing from her if he allowed her into his life. So thank goodness he was safe in the knowledge that he could give her no more than a night. If she wanted even that from him.

'I like looking at you,' she admitted, this time not darting her gaze away.

'Hailey—' He realised he didn't know what to say to her. How to ask for what he wanted, but not all of it. That he wanted tonight, and if things had been different he would probably want many nights after that, but that wasn't his to offer.

'Do you want to go upstairs?' she asked.

He was undoubtedly the most beautiful man she had seen in her life. She had suspected it that afternoon, when he had been stubbled and crumpled and jet-lagged, yawning through their meeting. In a clean shirt, freshly shaved, hair swept back off his forehead, he was devastating. And looking at her as if she were dessert.

She didn't have the chance to bed a living god very often. It seemed churlish to turn down the opportunity when it presented itself. When she'd been telling him the names of the flowers she had seen at her first flower market, his eyes had burned with intensity as she'd named more and more obscure specimens, exaggerating the shape of her lips around the long, twisting words. He could be a gift to herself, she reasoned. A little bonus for landing the biggest job of her career. For making a life for herself here in New York. She could play fairy tale princess with this beautiful man just for one night, knowing that was all it was. He could hardly be free to date a glorified flower seller, so there was no risk in taking what she wanted, just this once.

But he hadn't answered her. She looked across and felt the first pang of doubt. Had she misread this entirely, and he didn't want her after all?

Until he spluttered, 'Yes,' and stood abruptly.

She laughed into her wine. 'I didn't mean right this second.'

But he held his hand out to her. 'What's wrong with right this second?' he asked, and Hailey had to concede that he'd made a very good point.

She calmly set down her wine, pushed back her chair and stood. 'Lead the way then. We can order dessert upstairs.'

It was still dark when Hailey woke and eased out of Gio's arms, desperately tempted to stay under the blankets with him and say a proper goodbye. But she had to be at her workshop by seven or her team would have to condition that morning's delivery of flowers by themselves, and she'd always sworn to be the sort of boss who remembered how to roll up her sleeves and do even the least glamorous jobs herself.

Gio blinked sleepily a couple of times as she pulled on underwear and searched the suite for her clothes. 'Are you leaving?' he asked, his voice rough from lack of sleep as he levered himself up in bed and rested back against a heap of crumpled pillows.

Hailey smiled and crossed back to the bed, giving in and allowing herself to be pulled back down beside him, moaning lightly when his hands slipped into her hair and he pressed a gentle kiss to her lips.

'Good morning,' she said softly, between kisses. 'Sorry, I was trying not to disturb you. I have to get to work.'

'I don't mind you disturbing me like this,' Gio said, his hands sliding up her thighs. She smiled, not sure whether she should be more happy or sad that Gio had turned out to be an absolute sweetheart, who she wouldn't ever see again.

'Mmm…' she agreed, before pulling herself away again. 'But any more of that and I'm going to end up being late.' She glanced at her watch. 'Later than I already am. I'm going to have to go back to my place and change,' she observed, zipping up the black shift dress that she had worn to dinner last night.

'Here,' Gio said, snagging his shirt from the floor by the bed. 'How much time does it buy me if you wear this?' he asked. Hailey rolled her eyes but smiled as she pushed her arms into the sleeves and tried to roll up the cuffs, giving her wrists up to Gio to finish the job when he tugged at her hands.

'Find me something warm to wear over the top and you've got yourself twenty minutes,' she told him as he rolled the second one into place, only half joking. But Gio seemed to take it as a challenge. He kissed her hard once, and then disappeared into the walk-in closet.

'What are you doing?' she called out to him, resenting the fact that he was spending the last few minutes they had together separated by a door, rather than carrying on kissing her. She was on her way to tell him that when he emerged from the closet with an ice-blue sweater that looked so soft it had to be cashmere. He held it out to her and she hesitated for a moment before taking it. A swiped shirt was one thing—a classic walk of shame move. But this...this felt too much like a gift. Too intimate. But Gio slipped his fingers between the buttons of his shirt that she was wearing and pulled her to him. She looked up as he slipped the sweater over her head and tweaked the collar out of the neckline.

She pushed her arms in and pulled the body down—it slouched over one shoulder and hit mid-thigh—fitting better than any sweater dress she'd worn before. 'I can't take this,' she told him softly, rubbing the hem between thumb and finger. It was just as soft as she had imagined, and must have been more expensive than anything she owned.

For a moment, standing there in his clothes, enveloped in his scent, the morning light creeping through the window hitting cheekbones and jaw and early morning stubble all just right, she wished—just for a moment—that this could be the start of something. That she could promise to return his sweater that night, the perfect excuse to see him again. And at the same time she knew that she absolutely could not do that. She didn't belong in his world any more than he did in hers, and she was kidding herself if she thought that things could ever be any different.

'It's a gift,' Gio said, tilting her chin up so that she met his eyes. 'Looks better on you than it does on me anyway,' he said, giving her such a boyish grin that she couldn't help the chuckle that escaped her.

'Fine then,' she said. 'You've got yourself twenty minutes. What are you going to do with them?'

CHAPTER THREE

IT WAS STUPID to be awkward, after everything, Hailey told herself as she stood outside the door to Gio's hotel suite two months later. She'd had to send a very awkward text to Alexandra, Sebastian and Ivy's wedding planner, to confirm that Gio was staying in the same suite as the last time he'd been in town. Knocking on the door couldn't possibly be any worse than that, she told herself. After all, things hadn't been awkward when she and Gio had parted after the night they'd spent together. Far from it: they'd exchanged kisses but not phone numbers, both sleep-deprived but deeply satisfied, with no plans to see each other again, except in a strictly professional capacity.

And that was exactly how things would have stayed, if she didn't have this one, fairly important, piece of news to share with him. She should really knock on the door. The wedding was in three days, and she had no idea how long he would be in town after that. She needed to tell Gio face to face, before he left and she never saw him again.

She lifted her hand and rapped her knuckles on the wood before she could change her mind. As she waited for him to answer, she steeled herself for the surprise she'd see on his face. It had been so obvious to them both that they could be nothing more than a one-night stand that they'd never even felt the need to spell it out. And now she was showing up on his doorstep with news that would change his life. One way or another.

She knew how that felt—the experience was still raw. It had been only ten days since she had taken the pregnancy test, after a mad scramble back through her diary had shown her she'd missed not one but two periods since that night with Gio. She'd been so busy with all the preparations for Ivy and Sebastian's wedding that she hadn't even noticed.

Ten days was not enough time for the shock to fade. Not enough time to prepare herself for this conversation. But she'd seen the schedule for the wedding party between now and the big day, and there wasn't a minute free after this morning. And the news that you were going to be a father needed more than a minute to process. It needed more than ten days—she could attest to that—but she would take what she could get. He was going to take this badly, she knew, but she'd deal with that when the time came.

She rapped on the door of his suite a second time and could barely take a breath while she waited for him to answer. She wasn't even sure what she would do if he wasn't there. If someone else answered the door. If he had company. At least she knew he didn't have a date for the wedding—not that she'd looked at the guest list *just* to check that fact.

But he answered the door before she could have second thoughts and it was as if they had been cast back two months in time to that first afternoon they had met, when he had been rumpled and jet-lagged. This time he was barefoot and still had the creases from his pillow on his cheek, and he looked so... soft that she wanted to reach out and touch him.

But she mustn't. Because this situation was going to be difficult enough to negotiate without letting sex get in the way of things. Again. Nothing about their relationship had changed. Apart from the fact that they were having a child together. She had considered whether continuing with the pregnancy was the right choice, but after being abandoned as a baby by parents who didn't want her she couldn't imagine doing anything but meeting her baby with love and devotion.

She didn't expect Gio to feel the same way.

She didn't have to be told that a prince didn't get free choice over his life. And that an illegitimate child conceived during a one-night stand was the sort of thing that one covered up rather than celebrated. But he was the baby's father and it wasn't her place to make that decision for him, just to brace herself for it when it came and devote herself to loving her baby so much that it would never feel the lack of its other parent.

Gio's eyes widened as he rubbed sleep out of them with the heel of one hand. 'Hailey? What are you—?'

He seemed to remember those impeccable manners of his and pulled himself more upright before standing to one side, gesturing into the room with one arm.

'Come in, please. This is a pleasant surprise,' he lied, a polite, false smile on his face. He obviously thought that she was here to pick up where they had left off. Which under other circumstances would be somewhat mortifying. But, as it happened, was just… Yes.

Still mortifying. She straightened her spine and walked into his suite.

'So, Hailey, to what do I owe the—?'

She turned to look at him, standing in front of the door that he'd just closed behind her, and she took a moment to feel sympathy for him. Standing there in all innocence, with no idea of what was coming, thinking that this was just an awkward encounter with a ghost who hadn't understand his very clear message about their lack of future.

'I'm pregnant,' she blurted. She had planned to lead into it a little more gently, but he was looking at her as if he was preparing himself to put her out of her misery, and she couldn't bear to be the subject of his pity. Not even for a moment.

'You…' His stance was suddenly rigid, his body a stiff line in front of the door. 'You're pregnant?' he asked, and she nodded, giving him a moment to process the news.

'With my baby?' Fair question—he barely knew her. Had no reason to know that he was the only man she had been with in the last half a year, never mind in the last two months.

'Yes,' she said, holding her ground in front of the table in the lobby of the suite. The freesias were fresh, she noted out of habit, their scent familiar and comforting.

'I think we had better sit down,' Gio said, as shell-shocked as she had expected him to sound. She gave a sharp nod and followed him through to the sitting room, where she perched on the edge of an antique sofa, waiting for him to speak.

'This is a…surprise,' he said at last, and she couldn't help it, she laughed.

'For me too,' she offered, and for the first time a smile turned up the corner of his lips. It wasn't one of the grins that she'd basked in that night, a grin that used every facial muscle and left her somewhat dazzled. But it was something.

'How long have you known?' he asked.

'About a week and a half,' she said, her voice flat. 'I would have called, but I didn't have your number.'

'No. I suppose it's the sort of news one is meant to hear in person.' He nodded, and she wondered how much of this was sinking in and how much he was simply on autopilot. 'Thank you for telling me. I'm assuming you want to—'

'Keep it?' she interrupted, not wanting him to think that the alternative was on the cards. 'Yes, I do. I am. Of course, I understand that you probably don't want…'

'I do want,' he said, before she could outline exactly how she thought that he was going to let her down. And she was speechless with shock. He rubbed his face with his hands and there it was again, that sympathy for the fact that she was upending his world when he was jet-lagged and rumpled from sleep. If there was any good time to deliver news like this, this definitely wasn't it.

'I will be a father to the baby,' he said decisively, sitting on the sofa beside her and reaching out a hand, before seeming to change his mind and resting his forearms on his knees. 'Please do not doubt that.'

'I... I'm surprised,' she said, not thinking, and Gio narrowed his eyes at her.

'I didn't realise you thought so little of me.'

Hailey shook her head. 'I didn't. I don't,' she said, backtracking. 'I'm sorry for making assumptions. But in the circumstances...'

'What circumstances?'

There he went again, making her laugh when she had every intention of being serious. 'What circumstances? You mean apart from you being a prince, so not exactly the master of your own fate. You have obligations. You don't need to tell me that you're not free to... The baby was conceived during a one-night stand we had no intention of repeating. Oh, and we live on different continents. Other than those circumstances, you mean?'

He smiled, and she fought against the dazzling effect, knowing that those instincts weren't remotely helpful or relevant to this conversation.

'But we're going to have a baby,' Gio said, a touch of wonder making it through the shock in his voice.

She nodded, feeling slightly shell-shocked herself.

'We're having a baby,' she repeated, the first time that she'd said the words out loud. The first time the pregnancy had felt real.

'Then everything else comes second to that,' Gio said. 'Second to you, and the baby.' He reached for her hand, and this time she let him take it. 'We deal with this together,' he said, his voice low. 'We're a team now. A family.'

A family. He had wondered all his life what a family life would mean for him, and never once had he imagined this, that it would mean having a child with a partner he had chosen himself. Of course, they hadn't precisely chosen this. This was a wonderful accident that in an instant had changed the direction of his life. But he couldn't tell Hailey that. Couldn't tell her that having a baby with her undid all the plans that his parents had ever made for him. All the expectations that they had for his life. All the things that he was meant to do out of duty for his country, his family.

Well, everyone at the palace was simply going to have to come to terms with the fact that he wasn't going to be told how his life unfolded any more. He didn't know what the future looked like, but for the first time in his life he had the feeling that he could actually be the person who got to decide on its direction, and that was more than he had ever hoped for before.

'And are you well?' he asked Hailey, trying to remember that the fact that she was carrying his baby didn't change anything between the two of them. He had no right to expect that there would be any repeat of the night that had got them into this situation. Heaven knew she had made it clear enough the morning after that she didn't want to see him again, except in a professional capacity at the wedding. But surely a baby changed things? He had been equally sure that they would go their separate ways, no matter how often his thoughts had strayed in her direction in the weeks since they had been together.

So now what? His first thought had been

that his parents couldn't force him into a marriage now—who would take him with an illegitimate child in tow, complicating the succession as well as his private life? His brain caught on the word illegitimate. A bastard child would be shunned by his family, would have no claim to a part of its father's life.

He thought about that for a moment. How his life might have been different if he had been able to grow up away from the palace, and all the pressures it brought with it. And then he remembered the stark loneliness of his childhood—the feeling that he'd had every time his nanny had told him that his half hour with his parents was up and it was time to go to bed. He wouldn't do that to his child, leave them wondering whether their parents even loved him. He would make sure there was always a place in the palace for his child. That they always knew that they were loved. He wouldn't repeat his parents' mistakes.

'I'm fine, Gio,' Hailey said, and he remembered he had asked her that question. 'But are you?' Those pixie-like eyes were assessing him carefully, and he wondered how much the wounds of his childhood were on show.

'I'm fine,' he said automatically, because

he wasn't sure he had the vocabulary to tell her how he was really feeling. It was hard enough to understand, never mind explain, either in her language or his.

'I should give you some space,' Hailey said gently. 'It's a lot to take in, I know that. You probably need some time to get used to the idea.'

He nodded, because there was nothing that she had said that he could argue with. He could hardly gather his thoughts just now; there were too many of them, sprinting off in different directions.

'Let's talk tomorrow,' he said, because there was no way that he could wait longer than that to see her again.

'I've seen the schedule for tomorrow,' Hailey said, shaking her head. 'You can't possibly have the time.'

'I'll make time,' Gio said. 'This is more important. Tell me when is good for you and we can meet here.'

Hailey nodded and he breathed a sigh of relief; he hadn't realised until that moment that he'd been worried that she wouldn't agree to see him again.

Well, that could have gone worse, she supposed as she walked away from the hotel. He at least hadn't thrown her out of the room or refused to believe that the baby was his—or existed at all, all of which had crossed her mind. Turned out having a baby with a man you barely knew was full of unknowns, and it was hard to see where the next strike might be coming from.

But she had seen from the expression on Gio's face that he wasn't ready to talk about this yet—they had seven more months to get on top of the practicalities, so they could wait until tomorrow to start talking about it, if that was what he needed.

CHAPTER FOUR

GIO STRAIGHTENED THE cuffs of his shirt while he waited for Hailey to arrive. He had never felt this nervous before in his life but, then again, he had never had so much riding on the answer to one single question before either. His jet lag had kept him awake long into the night, and he'd had ample time to think in the silent small hours about how he could do right by both Hailey and their baby. And after following their choices through twisting labyrinths of possible futures it had become clear what he needed to do next.

He heard Hailey's efficient knock at the door—two sharp raps of her knuckle on the wood, and something deep in his stomach lurched with nerves. This was fine, he told himself. This was his choice. This hadn't been forced on him by Hailey, his family or anyone else. He wasn't trapped—he was choosing this for himself. If he told himself that often enough, maybe he'd even start to believe it. Because he might be choosing this *now*, but it was hardly a free choice, not now the baby was on the way. Without that complication, he'd chosen the exact opposite, walking away from Hailey and everything that she had made him feel. The melancholy he had felt, knowing that he could never live a life where he was in control of his destiny. Where he could make actual choices about his future, free from the constraints of his position.

'Come in, you look lovely,' Gio said as he answered the door to Hailey, remembering at the last moment that this was supposed to be a happy occasion. He'd added the compliment on autopilot, but as he said it he realised how true the words were. Her cheeks and lips were rosy pink, her hair framing her face in soft, shiny waves. And she glowed in the way he'd heard expectant mothers did, but had never actually seen for himself before.

'So, I suppose we have a lot to talk about,' Hailey said over her shoulder as they walked to the same sofa where she had sat yesterday. Hailey perched on the edge, her posture the very definition of composed. The whole scene couldn't be more different to the night that they had stumbled up here from the restaurant, when the only things that had landed on these seats were items of clothing tossed there en route to the bedroom.

Life would be so much easier if he could simply forget that night. If they could approach this impending co-parenting without all those memories muddying the water. But his brain had the unfortunate habit of throwing graphic memories at him at the most unhelpful moments. Like now, when he was meant to be proposing, and instead he was remembering the taste of the skin on Hailey's neck, warm and salty with perspiration.

'I appreciate that the distance is going to make things complicated, but I'm sure that we can work out a way for you to have regular visitation with the baby.'

'Visitation?' he asked, taken aback by Hailey seeming to already be half way through a conversation.

'Yes,' Hailey said, and he saw her composure falter for a second before she reined herself back in. 'Yesterday, you said that you wanted to be involved in the baby's life. Of course, if you've changed your mind…'

'I've not changed my mind,' Gio said quickly, because that was the furthest thing from what he wanted. 'I don't want to just "visit" my own child. I want… I want to marry you, Hailey. I want you to come back to Adria with me.'

* * *

She wasn't sure how long they sat there in silence while she sorted through the various warring thoughts clamouring in her brain. The idea that she should marry Gio was ridiculous, of course. For so many reasons that she couldn't just this second decide which of them she wanted to remind Gio of.

They lived continents apart.

He was a prince. She was a commoner.

It was meant to be a one-night stand.

They barely knew each other.

He was clearly acting out of some well-intentioned chivalry, which was admirable but not the recipe for a happy marriage. Not if he felt that he was being strong-armed into it.

'I don't want to,' she blurted out, a little more directly than she had intended. And she was surprised to see his face fall with disappointment. Did he actually want to do this?

Even if that was the case, it didn't make the idea any less absurd. You didn't marry someone you barely knew just because you'd got pregnant. This was the twenty-first century.

And yet. There was something so appealing about the thought. Nothing to do with the palace or the money. Or, God forbid, the interest from the press. No, it was the idea of them being a family—the type with two parents and a baby they desperately loved. All living together, all wanting to be together. She didn't want to be a princess, she didn't want to think about the implications of joining a family like Gio's, but she did want...that.

The problem was, she couldn't have one without the other.

'Gio, I'm sorry, that came out more bluntly than I'd intended. I only meant to say that I don't want to marry out of obligation. Or for convenience. I... The thought of being a proper family for this baby is incredibly tempting. And I'm touched that you would want that enough to propose. But let's be sensible. I don't fit into your world. I'm never going to fit into your world. It just makes more sense for us to go about our lives as before. I know that you will make time for the baby. I trust you to be a good father.'

Gio leaned forward, elbows resting on his knees. 'I want to be more than a good father,' he said. 'I want to be *there*. I don't want to miss any of it. And the only way to do that is to live together. I understand that you have a life here and I respect that. But if you come to Adria we can make opportunities for you there too. I can help with that, with connections. Or if you don't want to work you don't have to—or we'll divide our time between

Adria and New York, until…until my obligations mean that I can't be so often out of the country. Just…think about it. Please?'

She thought about it for a second, her eyes fixed on his clasped hands. 'We could do all of that without being married,' she pointed out, and he dropped his head into his hands.

'But I have to marry,' he said, his voice muffled before he looked up and met her gaze. 'I've always known that. Discussions about who I would marry started before I could walk. My parents will be no less firm on the issue even if I have a baby with you. Adria will need a legitimate heir…'

'What, and I'm the brood mare? How flattering.'

'No, that's not what I mean at all. But my parents won't stop their pressure just because we have a child together. The thought of marrying for Adria has always been…'

She watched him search for the word, and felt a wave of sympathy for him.

'Challenging. The thought of having to do it while you and our child are treated differently would be unthinkable. But, given your condition, my parents can't object publicly to our marriage without causing a scandal. And if we are married they can't force me to marry anyone else.'

'Gio,' she said softly, reaching for his hand. 'No one can force you to get married.'

'No,' he agreed. 'But they can make their disapproval clear if I do not go along with their intentions.'

'And is their disapproval so important, if they don't care enough about your feelings to recognise that they are hurting you?'

'They're my family.'

She nodded. She'd never thought that she could feel sorry for a man raised in a palace but, from the sound of it, his childhood had created emotional wounds every bit as deep as the ones that she had been carrying.

It was all too much—too much to think about and too much decide while she was sitting here looking at him. This close, it was hard to know what she was thinking and feeling, never mind making a good decision about her future. Especially as it wasn't just *her* future at stake. She was a mother now, and she had to make the right decision for her baby too.

'I... I need to think about this, Gio. I didn't expect this.'

'You're pregnant with my baby and it never occurred to you that the sensible thing is to get married?'

'No.' She shook her head and sat up a little

straighter. 'Because I don't live in the nine-teenth century. I'm not some fallen woman you need to rescue.'

'No. But I'm a public figure with a coun-try's reputation depending on my choices and my decisions.'

'Wow. An obligatory proposal. You do know how to make a girl feel special. So how does it work?' she asked. 'We smile for the cameras on our wedding day, then go to our separate wings of the palace while you discreetly smuggle a mistress in through the kitchens?'

'I would never...'

'Never? Really? Because, if not, you're making a lot of assumptions about what would be included in this marriage of con-venience. How long do you normally go with-out—?'

'No one said anything about a marriage of convenience.'

His words fell into heavy silence.

'Of course you meant a marriage of conve-nience,' Hailey said, refusing to let her voice shake. 'You only asked me to marry you be-cause I'm pregnant.'

'Yes,' he agreed. 'Of course that's true. But you're pregnant because...we had a con-nection. More than a physical connection, I mean. We spent the night together because we were enjoying each other's company at dinner. I just think that we should remember that, if we can. But, right now, we have to decide a few things. We need to think about how this will look to everyone,' he said, changing the subject. 'If we don't make a pitch for how this story is reported then someone else will. And they won't run it past us first.'

'Your family?'

'Perhaps. If we're lucky. Depends on how quickly they move and whether the press pick up on it from somewhere else first. Does anyone else know?'

'You're the first person I've told,' she said.

'Good.'

'Good?' Hailey stiffened. 'Good because you're going to be a father and you're happy that you're the first to know it? Or good because I haven't pre-emptively scuppered your public relations campaign?'

He sat up straighter, his tense posture mirroring her own. 'You're being naïve,' he told her.

'Excuse me?' Hailey spluttered, unable to believe he could accuse her of that. '*I'm* being naïve? You're the one who thinks that getting married is going to solve this, rather than making it a million times more complicated.'

Shaking his head, Gio said, 'I apologise. I shouldn't have said that.'

'If you're already thinking it,' Hailey said, 'whether you say it out loud or not is neither here nor there.'

Gio collapsed against the back of the sofa and ran a hand through his hair, leaving it more dishevelled than ever. 'I feel very much that we have got off on the wrong foot,' he said, his voice softer and more conciliatory than she had heard it before, and she cracked a little smile.

'*I* feel we got off very much on the right foot and that's what got us into this situation in the first place.'

Gio returned her smile and his face was transformed by it, every muscle working to show her exactly what he was feeling.

'Yes. Well. That much is true, I'm sure,' he said.

'I'm flattered, Gio, that you think I could be a part of your world. But it wouldn't work. And I'm sorry that I can't accept your proposal.'

She watched him in silence for a moment, and then two, as her words struck home, and wished she could know what he was thinking. His feelings played out so clearly on his face when he was pleased; his smiles were illuminating in so many ways. But his other feelings were too well masked, too disguised for her to be able to interpret them.

'I think, Hailey, that whether you accept my proposal or not, you're a part of my world now. You're the mother of my child and that makes you family. And, while I wouldn't wish my family on anyone, here we are. Of course you need time, I understand that. But I'm not sure how much we have to work with. I fly back to Adria the day after the wedding.'

'That's three days,' she reminded him. 'We can't make a decision like that in three days.'

'Then come to Adria,' he protested. 'Spend some time with me. See how things are if we get to know each other. At least give it a chance before you rule it out completely.'

'What are you thinking?' he asked after a long silence, and she wondered what was showing on her face.

She took a deep breath. 'I was just thinking…it would be nice for the baby, you know. A nuclear family. I wish that was something that we could give him. Or her.'

Gio grimaced, the expression so different from one of his smiles. 'You've not met my parents. There's not a lot in my experience to recommend the nuclear family.'

'Yes, well, I can only attest to the opposite, and that didn't have much going for it either.'

She stood abruptly, not wanting to delve into her family history with Gio as a witness, and aware that she had already said too much.

Gio stood, following her, and the action brought his body to within a stride of hers. It would be so easy, so comforting, to take that step and rest her head on his chest. She could accept his proposal and ignore the fact that it was just for show and give her baby the family life that she had never had. Or maybe he would take a step towards her and take the decision out of her hands.

'Hailey, I've upset you. I apologise,' he said, not coming any closer.

She shook her head and fought to regain her composure. 'No, you haven't. I just need to go. I have a lot to do for the wedding.'

Gio reached out a hand and brushed it, just briefly, against her elbow. 'We need to talk again.'

She nodded. 'We will. Of course. Let's just take a couple of days to gather our thoughts. Decide what we want.'

'And in the meantime—'

'I know. Don't tell anyone.'

'No. That's not what I was going to say.' And he took just half a step. Coming too close, but not close enough. Standing near enough to her that she had to tip her head back to look him in the eye, but not offering the oblivion of burying her face into his body to block out the rest of the world. 'In the meantime, if you need anything...if you're not well or you need to talk. *Anything*, Hailey, promise me that you will call me.'

He pulled out a card from the inside pocket of his jacket, scribbled a phone number on the back and passed it to her. 'We're together in this, okay? I don't want you to question that, whatever happens. I am truly delighted by this news. I hope you know that, however complicated it may feel at this moment.'

Delighted. Such a word, and he was; it showed in every muscle on his face. She wondered if that smile would ever not dazzle her. Would her—their—baby inherit that smile? She could imagine a very spoiled child in her future if it did.

'I'm happy that you are. And I am too.' She smiled back at him, though it was a poor reflection of his.

Hailey watched from a shadowy corner at the back of the ballroom as Gio gave his toast to the happy couple. She should probably have left already—once she had checked that the table centrepieces were perfect, there was nothing flower-related left for her to do. And yet here she was, watching Gio and the rest of the wedding party, surrounded by fairy lights and her beautiful flowers and the shimmering Christmas decorations that had transformed the room into a fairy tale, and she couldn't walk away.

Parker and Parker had been at the top of her list of dream venues to work with since she'd heard that it would be hosting weddings, and it was decorated beautifully for Christmas. From the towering trees, dusted with snow and strung with ice-white lights, that lined the steps up to the entrance of the building, to the crystal chandeliers in the grand foyer, garlanded with pine and white poinsettias, and branches strung with lights, like stars seen through the arms of bare winter trees, every inch of it had been transformed into an opulent Christmas fantasy.

The elegant design of every aspect of the day tied together perfectly, from the hand-tied, lace-trimmed bouquets that Hailey had passed to Ivy and her bridesmaids that morning, to the towering arrangements in the ballroom and the carefully designed centrepieces for the tables, which added texture and drama without getting in the way of the conversation the room now hummed with.

The bride swept through the crowd in her floor-length white gown, bewitching everyone who looked in her direction. Not least of whom her groom, with his immaculate tuxedo and besotted expression. They held the attention of every person present. Except Hailey, who had spent half her afternoon watching out for Gio and the other half chastising herself for doing so.

But when Gio stood up to give his toast and the eyes of the whole room fell on him, she gave herself permission to fall in with the crowd. To look properly at him, just for a few minutes. And once he started speaking she couldn't help but wonder what he might say on their wedding day, if she accepted his proposal. Certainly he wouldn't be speaking about love, as he was able to about the couple beside him, who were looking at each other adoringly.

Perhaps he would mention duty or obligation. Family and country.

And she had to stop a sigh escaping, knowing that their marriage could only ever be a shadow of the happiness that she had witnessed today.

Hailey finally sank into bed at midnight, with tired feet and an aching back, and it felt as if she had barely closed her eyes when she heard a rap on the door. She glanced at the clock beside the bed. It was somehow six in the morning. She shook her head, trying to shake the fatigue that seemed to have settled into her bones this week. She stumbled to the door and opened it a crack, realising too late that she was wearing an oversized man's shirt that barely skimmed her thighs.

'Gio?' she asked, confused, as she took in the sight of him on the other side of the door. 'It's six in the morning.' Either it was six in the morning and a crown prince really was standing outside her front door or she was dreaming. The dreaming seemed so much more likely, but the gust of cold air on her legs felt all too real.

'I'm sorry,' Gio said. 'Jet lag. I thought I would have heard from you before now and I was going a little crazy. We have so little time. I fly back to Adria tonight and couldn't go without knowing...'

'I've been so busy...' she said, as if that was the real reason she hadn't been in touch.

'I know.' Gio nodded. 'I understand. But I have to get on that plane tonight and I can't bear the thought of doing that without more certainty. I want you to come with me. Just... will you come for a walk with me? I brought coffee. There's regular or decaf. I didn't know which you want.'

'At six in the morning? You can keep your decaf.'

'Understood. Please, I think it might snow. I've been here four days and haven't seen anything of the city. Will you show it to me?'

She glanced past him up and down the street, to make sure they were alone. 'You should come in. I'll get dressed.'

'I'll wait here. Give you some privacy.'

'And have someone see you hanging outside my apartment? I don't think so. Come in. But turn your back.'

She tugged the hem of her shirt down, hoping that he wouldn't notice it was the one he had given her, which had somehow become her regular nightshirt, as she opened the door a fraction wider and took the coffees from him.

'You know, I think I'll need both of these,' she said as a waft of coffee reached her.

'Maybe we should do this later,' Gio said, hesitating on the threshold.

'You already woke me. I'll never get back to sleep. The least you can do is entertain me.'

She disappeared into her bedroom and returned wearing jeans that wouldn't quite button—for a very obvious reason—and swathed in layers, more than ready for anything that a New York winter could throw at her—the snow had been coming down heavily when she'd gone to bed last night—because what she was wearing was something that she could control.

Hat, scarf, mittens? Check. Decisions about her future with the father of her child? No idea what she was doing.

From the corner of her eye she caught Gio smiling at her and threw him a look. 'What?' she asked.

'Nothing. You're just…' She raised an eyebrow, waiting. 'I feel like there might be a strong reaction if I say adorable,' Gio went on hesitantly.

'There will be a violent reaction if you say adorable,' she confirmed, tossing cushions and looking for her phone before finding it plugged into her charger, right where she'd left it the night before.

Gio took a step towards her as she slipped her phone into her pocket, and when she looked up he was close—very close. She craned her neck to look up at him.

'You are very…little,' he said with a quirk of his lips, tucking a strand of hair behind her ear. 'I could just pick you up and…'

She took a step backwards, raising her eyebrows at him. 'Too complicated,' she said firmly. 'I can't think and make decisions if you're saying things like that. If you're looking at me like that.'

Gio shook his head, taking a step away too. 'I'm sorry. I wasn't thinking. You're right. That would be very complicated indeed.'

She agreed, trying to convince herself as much as him. 'If we're going to get married, I don't know if I can handle any more complications on top of that just now.'

'*If* we're going to get married?' he asked, and she couldn't decide if he sounded more shocked or hopeful.

She pulled the door to the apartment building open and gasped as the cold air from outside hit her. A flurry of snow blew into the hallway before she managed to pull the door closed. She took one of the coffees from Gio and warmed her hands around the cup as she crunched through a pile of ice on the sidewalk, carefully watching where she was putting her feet. If she looked at Gio directly, she wasn't going to be able to do this.

'Yes. I want this baby to know its family,' she said. 'To be a part of it. Properly. And if family means parents who are married to each other then that's what is going to happen.'

She had gone round and round in circles,

trying to think of a way to give her baby everything that she had missed out on in her childhood, and hadn't been able to come up with anything other than this—marry Gio, give her baby what it deserved and worry about her own feelings for the father at some unspecified point in the future, which she was sure would be simpler and provide more opportunity for introspection. Surely, visiting the country of which the father of your unborn baby was Crown Prince would provide ample opportunity for quiet contemplation.

They stopped to cross the road and she had to squint through the snow to see the light on the other side of the crossing. Gio's hand came to rest on her elbow and she fought down her instinct to shake him off, reasoning that it was sensible to accept help when she was walking through snow in the dark.

Pulling her hat lower on her head, she led him through the park on the corner of her street, with its railings lined with fairy lights, bows hanging from the lamp-posts and a towering Christmas tree in the centre.

They walked in thoughtful silence through the quiet early-morning streets, only stopping to admire an illuminated courtyard in the narrow space between two buildings which had been decorated with multicoloured strings of lights and an illuminated wreath on the gates.

'I'll need some time to pack,' Hailey said quietly as they stood at the railings and took in the festive display. 'And I'll probably have to run to a store for a few things, depending on how long we'll be staying. Oh, I have an appointment scheduled with an ob-gyn next week.'

Gio turned to look at her, his hand slipping from her elbow to her hand, and she forced herself to take a step away.

'Of course,' Gio said. 'I need to fly out tonight. You can take all the time you want. But anything you need I can arrange for you in Adria, including a doctor, if you wish. I don't want you to be…inconvenienced.'

A laugh burst out of her. 'Inconvenienced?' she said, her voice bordering on wild. 'You got me *pregnant*, Gio,' she said, still trying to get her breath back because she was laughing so hard. 'You don't want to inconvenience me?' she repeated, wheezing with laughter.

Gio stepped in front of her and crossed his arms, staring down at her. 'You're laughing at me.'

'I'm not, I'm not,' Hailey said, trying to get her breathing—and her laughter—under control. 'I'm laughing at the situation. It's absurd. You said it yourself. And tonight we're going to get on a plane and nothing is ever going to be the same. How do we do this? Will we see your family tonight? Go straight to the palace?'

Gio thought about it for a moment. 'Yes,' he replied eventually. 'If you agree. We should tell them as soon as possible and I want to do it in person.'

Hailey nodded and Gio reached for her hand, brushing the back of it with his thumb before pulling away. He took a deep breath and forced it out through his teeth. 'They're going to be angry,' he said, and her stomach lurched even as she was grateful for his honesty. 'Don't misunderstand me; they will be unfailingly polite to you. It's me they'll be disappointed with. But they won't let anyone else see that.'

'I'm not worried about how they are with me,' Hailey said, feeling brave. 'They're nothing to me, to be perfectly honest. I've never been interested in their opinion of me before, and I haven't heard anything that makes me think their good opinion is worth having. It's not me I'm worried about. It's you.'

'You don't have to worry about me,' Gio said as they turned and walked on, and he forced a smile that was almost painfully lacklustre. They had reached Twenty-Eighth Street and Hailey couldn't help but be happy to be around the familiar sounds and scents of the flower district. She felt more at home in this short stretch of New York City than in any home she'd ever occupied in the UK. Every time she walked these sidewalks, she knew exactly who she was and what she wanted for her life. Except now, with Gio beside her, all those old certainties were gone.

'I might not have to worry, but I'm going to anyway,' Hailey said, sidestepping around a pile of planters and pots, forcing her closer to Gio's side. She made her voice soft, despite the anger that she felt. 'Because, frankly, it sounds like your parents are cruel.'

Gio shook his head. 'They're not cruel.'

She felt her heart ache for him a little, that he could be treated so badly by the people who were meant to love him the most and not even recognise how much they were hurting him. 'You're scared to tell them that you're having a baby,' she told him gently. 'That doesn't sound like a loving and supportive relationship.'

'There's a difference between difficult and cruel.'

'Making you doubt that they care about you is cruel,' she told him. 'I've barely known you five minutes and I already know you would never treat our child like that, no matter the circumstances.'

'I'm glad you know that,' Gio said, stopping to let the fronds of a fern slip through his fingers, knocking away the flakes of snow they had been collecting. 'I know that this is unconventional,' he said. 'And I'm sure that there are a thousand reasons why we should be second-guessing ourselves. So really it's remarkable just how happy I am about this baby. Please try and remember that when we're in the midst of family politics.'

Family politics. Unfortunately, in his family, family politics tended to stumble into the arena of fragile international diplomacy, which he suspected he'd just thrown a brick through.

And his parents were going to treat him like a wayward ambassador rather than a cherished son who was delighting them with news of their first grandchild. He'd spent his whole life being treated as a slightly disappointing subject and was well able to handle it, but it wasn't fair to expect Hailey to have to put up with their nonsense. His parents had perfected the art of freezing someone out without ever, for a moment, breaching the rules of polite conversation. He would protect Hailey from it the best he could because he hadn't forgotten what she'd said about her own family, and how the lack of one had caused her pain. He knew that she was coming into this situation with scars of her own, and he wasn't going to let his parents hurt her.

CHAPTER FIVE

'So THIS IS your world,' Gio said, looking around the market. It was still snowing, though more lightly now, and flakes were catching in his hair and eyelashes. Prince Giovanni in the snow. It would be a fairy tale if there wasn't so much of her real life at stake.

He'd visited her in her workshop near here the first time she'd met him, but that had been late afternoon, which might as well have been the middle of the night as far as the early risers at the flower market were concerned. The stalls and stores had been practically deserted then, rather than how she loved them, how they were now, packed with people and flowers and foliage.

'This has been home, really,' she said, picking the stems of fern he'd been fingering from the bucket, adding some seeded eucalyptus, myrtle and cascading maidenhair fern into a tumbling bouquet of greenery. The store owner emerged from the building and handed her a length of twine with a raised eyebrow but without asking questions, and she wrapped it around the stems, fingers working with muscle memory, even through knitted mittens. She paid and thanked the store owner and then handed the bouquet to Gio, trying not to think too hard about what she was doing. For a moment, he just stared at her.

'I don't think anyone has ever given me flowers before,' he said, looking between the tied bundle and her face, a little dazed.

'Technically, it's just foliage,' Hailey said, deflecting. 'And you have good taste,' she added, feeling her cheeks pinken up. 'These ferns are lovely. Call it an engagement present.'

He almost stumbled at that, and she had to laugh softly as she grabbed his elbow. 'Having second thoughts?' she asked, not entirely sure that she was joking.

'No, absolutely not. It just reminded me, I wanted to talk to you. About a ring.'

She stopped and turned to him, her feet suddenly taking root. 'Oh, you don't have to… I wasn't hinting…'

'I didn't think for a second that you were,' Gio said, smoothing over her stumbling words. 'I really *have* been wanting to talk to you about it but I didn't want to press you. It's tradition to choose a family piece for the engagement ring. But I don't want to—'

'No, you're right, of course. This isn't even real. It wouldn't be appropriate—'

'Hailey. Stop. Please. Let me finish. Of course this is real. It may not be entirely conventional—though, given the history of European royal families, I rather think that the statistics might be on our side. We are the ones who decide what "real" looks like for us. I only brought it up because I want you to be able to choose. I don't want to stick you with some antique if it's not what you want. We could choose something new, either here or in Adria. Or something from the family collection together. I want to give you choices, Hailey.'

'Because you've never had any,' she said, seeing the root of the issue although she suspected he wasn't even aware of it.

'I didn't say that.'

'Seems you don't have to say things out loud for me to know what you're thinking.' Which was terrifying, for many reasons. Mainly because it was true, and a result of the absurd intimacy that had been so characteristic of their relationship from the start. Which she really shouldn't be dwelling on. She had said that things were too complicated, and she was right. She had to concentrate on the baby. Work out how she was meant to live in Gio's world. How she was meant to raise a baby in a world that she didn't understand. She'd thought she was done with that—with figuring out the rules of someone else's family and trying to make herself a part of it. She'd come here to New York, where she'd known she would stick out, where no one would expect her to know the rules. And somehow she'd found her place, found her people. Here on these streets that woke before dawn and were packing up for the day before noon. She'd found Gracie here, or Gracie had found her.

'There's someone I need you to meet,' she said suddenly. Before she could overthink it.

'Now?' Gio asked, laughing and looking at his watch. 'It's eight a.m.'

'So Gracie will be on her third pot of coffee. With any luck she'll be brewing number four and we can share.'

'Okay, pre-breakfast meeting then,' he said gamely. 'And Gracie is…?'

'She was my boss at my first job in New York. I worked part-time as a florist while I was at college. Gracie taught me everything I know about floristry, and most of what I know about myself. She's a…she's a really good friend.'

Though of course 'friend' wasn't nearly a big enough word for someone who meant so much to her. It was unthinkable that she could leave for Adria without telling Gracie her news. All of it.

She led Gio across the road and then pulled him through the door into Gracie's store. 'Gracie?' she called, guessing her friend was in the small room at the back where she hung the aprons and kept the coffee pot.

'Hailey, honey, is that you?' Gracie shouted back, before emerging through the curtain over the door, wrapping her arms around Hailey and squeezing her in a bone-crushing hug. 'This is a wonderful surprise! How did the wedding go yesterday?' the older woman asked. And then she looked past Hailey to Gio, who was still standing by the door. 'And who's this?' She held Hailey away from her by her upper arms and gave her a rather knowing look.

Hailey cleared her throat awkwardly. 'Yes, of course. Gracie, this is…' She hesitated over how exactly she was meant to introduce the Crown Prince who had got her pregnant. Until she remembered how simply Gio had introduced himself to her. 'Gracie, this is Gio.' She paused. 'We have a little news.'

Gracie glanced away from Hailey, over her shoulder to Gio, before her eyes locked back on Hailey's face. 'You have some news, huh?' Her eyes flicked down to Hailey's midriff, and she knew her friend had guessed correctly.

'We're expecting a baby,' she said quickly, getting the words out there. 'And we're getting married. I'm flying out to Adria tonight.'

'Well, honey, that's quite a *lot* of news,' Gracie said, her glance over Hailey's shoulder rather more suspicious now. 'If you'll excuse us...'

'Gio,' Hailey prompted her.

'If you'll excuse us, Gio, I need to speak to Hailey alone for a moment.'

Gracie's firm grip on her arm slipped down to her wrist as she tugged her into the back room.

Gracie fixed her with a look from which Hailey knew there was no escape. 'What's going on,' she demanded.

'I mean, I think I gave you the highlights,' Hailey said, trying—and failing—not to meet her eye.

'Uh-huh. You did. And now I want the small print. Is this what you want? I never even heard you mention this guy and now you're getting married. Leaving New York. Sweetheart, if you need help, you only have to ask. Not even that. Give me any sign that you want me to step in here and I'll keep you safe. You have options.'

Hailey let out a deep breath, because she knew Gracie meant it. If she was in trouble, Gracie would burn down buildings to get her out of it. Knowing that lifeline was there made it a little easier to breathe, even though she didn't need it.

'I know it's unexpected,' Hailey said, taking a seat on one of the stools by the counter, pouring them both a cup of coffee and opening the bag of pastries she knew she'd find in the drawer. 'It was the furthest thing from planned. But we're both excited about the baby, and we both want to try being a family.'

'Oh, honey, there are a lot of ways to be a family,' Gracie said, laying a hand on her arm. 'I know you know that.'

'I do, and I've tried many of them—including finding my own family in the New York flower district—and it's made me feel happier and more loved than I ever have in my life. But the only one I haven't tried is a family with a child being brought up by its birth parents, and this is my only chance to find out what that feels like.'

Gracie sighed. 'Just because that is more traditional it doesn't mean it's better, or that it will make you happy. You and Gio can make a good family without you giving up your life here.'

Hailey nodded, because she knew that Gracie was right. She also knew that she couldn't give up this opportunity to try. 'I know that. But we're still going to try.'

'Okay.' The older woman nodded thoughtfully. 'Then you should know that you have my full support and you always will, whatever happens.'

This time it was Hailey who hugged Gracie to her. 'Thank you. You have no idea what it means to me to hear you say that.'

Gracie sniffed, and Hailey wondered if she was close to tears too. 'Should we put the boy out of his misery? Or leave him to stew a little longer?' Gracie asked.

'Let's go back out there,' Hailey said. 'I'm half terrified that he's going to come to his senses and take it all back.'

'He'd have to be criminally stupid to do that. The way he looks at you, I don't think you have anything to worry about.'

'Oh, it's not—' she started to say, before she stopped herself. She had been going to say that this wasn't a real marriage. She didn't even know what it was. All she could be sure of was that she had to marry him, and it seemed safer altogether if she kept her feelings out of the equation. Falling for Gio could only make things more complicated, so she was simply going to forbid herself from doing so. 'We're very happy,' she said weakly.

When she returned from the back room, Gio was pacing with hands clasped behind his back, and Hailey was surprised and a little touched to see he looked nervous.

'Everything all right?' he asked Hailey, with a nervous glance at Gracie.

'Everything's great,' she told him, leaving Gracie's side and coming to stand beside him. And then, suddenly, it wasn't. She felt tears pricking the back of her eyes and she fought to keep her chin from juddering with held back tears. Because she was leaving. And as much as she wanted to give her child the family it deserved—and that meant Gio—it meant leaving the family she'd found here, after looking for so long.

'We don't have to go,' Gio said gently, tilting her face up with a knuckle under her chin.

'You already told me that you do. Your family.'

He brushed her hair back from her face,

cupped her cheek gently. 'So I'll call them. They'll get over it.'

She laughed a little at that. 'I know you don't mean that and we both know it's not so simple. But I appreciate the sentiment.'

'I do mean it. We've never really talked about what your leaving New York means. That was unforgivable of me.'

'So we'll talk about it in Adria,' she said. 'But we should go, tonight. Your parents are expecting you.'

'If you're sure.' He was focused one hundred per cent on her, his hands cupped at her cheeks, and it was hard resisting the urge to turn her head and nuzzle into his palm.

'I'm sure,' she said, her voice steadier. 'We can always come back. I hear those planes fly both ways across the Atlantic.'

He huffed a little laugh under his breath. 'Well, I flew back to you, didn't I?'

Hailey stared at him, aware that her expression must be turning goofy. But there was something about the way he'd said those words that made her stomach tighten. It almost sounded as if he meant it, that he was here with her because he wanted to be and not because the New York social calendar and a glitch in her contraception had forced them back into each other's lives.

She heard Gracie clear her throat behind her, and remembered that they weren't alone. When she turned around, Gracie was giving her a look that made her blush.

'You know, I don't think I need to worry about you after all. Enjoy your trip, honey. And let me know the minute you're back in New York. I want to know everything that happens with this baby. And I'm always at the end of the phone. If you need anything, you call me. You understand?'

She was gathered in to Gracie's chest for a hug and took the opportunity to surreptitiously wipe away a tear with the heel of one hand.

'I'll call. I promise. But you don't have to worry about me. I'm fine—I'm happy,' she said again with a self-conscious glance at Gio.

They left the store, back out onto the street, bracketed each side by towering bamboos and ferns, surrounded by blooms in holiday reds and whites and greens, all covered in snow. She had no idea what she was going to do away from this place. She had worked too hard to set up her business to just let it go because she was going to be a mother. And she couldn't just shut up shop in New York and start afresh in Adria. She had no clients there. No contacts. No suppliers. She employed a team of assistants here and she couldn't just fire them all because she'd decided to torch her life in New York.

She was going to be a princess, she reminded herself. She wasn't exactly an expert on European royalty, but she didn't know of any who were running their own business. As far as she was aware, if you didn't want to work for the family firm you got thrown out. They would have to talk about this, and soon. But they had to get the small question of telling his parents out of the way first. They'd deal with the practicalities of their lives first.

'So that went… Did that go well?' Gio asked. 'I feel like I'd need to know Gracie better to judge.'

Hailey smiled, bumping herself against his side. 'It went fine. I think she liked you.'

She stopped walking suddenly, as she spotted a poster on the building in front of them. It was for an exhibition at The Metropolitan Museum of Art, a painting that she had studied for her art history major, and that had inspired her first solo attempts at floristry. She remembered the first time that she had seen it, in a library book at her art school: there had been something about the way that the light caught on the flowers, the contrast of rich colours against a dramatically dark background, that had inspired something deep inside her. It had seemed magical. Otherworldly.

She had thought, *I have access to light. I have access to flowers. I want to make something that moves me like this painting does. But I want to be able to walk all around it. I want to be able to touch it, to smell it.* And she had worked with Gracie to find the flowers that she needed, and the best way to display them, and find the light that picked out their colours and their shadows.

'What is it?' Gio asked, interrupting her memory.

Hailey hesitated, not sure how honest she should be. She forced a smile and kept her voice light. 'Nothing, just an exhibition that I'd hoped to see. It doesn't start until next week and it's only running for a few days. There's a painting that I loved when I was at art school; I've never seen it properly. But it's fine. I'm sure I'll get another chance.'

She looked up at Gio, who was frowning.

'You definitely have to fly out tonight?' she asked, already knowing what the answer would be.

'My parents are expecting me.'

She shrugged off her disappointment and stopped outside another couple of stores as they walked along Twenty-Eighth Street.

'What time is the flight?' she asked. 'And how long should I be planning on staying? I need to know what to pack.'

'I'll have the car pick you up at eight to give us enough time to get to the airport. And as for how long? That's up to you. I'm inviting you to Adria. To visit. To live. But I don't want to force you into anything. We can decide together how long you want to stay. And if you change your mind and want to come back, you come straight back. If you haven't brought something that you need, then we'll get it for you in Adria.'

She nodded again. 'It's Christmas in ten days,' she said, trying to keep her voice casual. 'It'd look strange if we spent our first Christmas apart.'

Gio stopped, touched her hand lightly until she turned to him. 'We could fly back here if you want,' he said, his eyes serious.

'And have you take four transatlantic flights in less than a fortnight?' Hailey forced a smile. 'You'd be wrecked. No, we'll spend Christmas in Adria. Do we have to spend it with your family or...?'

'There's tradition. Church for Midnight Mass. Balcony photocall in the afternoon. Dinner with the family, of course.'

She nodded. It was what she'd expected. 'Okay, so we're going to be seeing a lot of them.'

'Normally I would. This year…' Gio ran a hand through his hair.

'You think we're going to be banished?'

'I think maybe we'll want some space from them,' he said diplomatically. 'Six hours around a dinner table might be a little much.'

'It's going to cause enough waves, me turning up pregnant, out of wedlock.'

'Not for long,' Gio argued.

'Excuse me?' Hailey frowned, unsure of his meaning.

'You're not going to be out of wedlock for long,' he clarified, running a hand through his hair.

'Right.' Hailey nodded. 'Of course.'

It still felt surreal. Not only was she pregnant, but she was going to be married soon. Married into a royal family, at that.

'We didn't really talk about a timescale for that,' she observed.

'Soon,' Gio said quickly. 'I want to do it soon.'

'Right. The closer to nine months after the wedding the baby arrives the better, I suppose. Though you know that I'm two months gone already.'

Gio's eyes met hers. 'That's not the reason.'

CHAPTER SIX

HE PROBABLY SHOULD have lied and said that of course that was the reason he wanted to marry quickly. She'd given him the perfect excuse, and he'd discarded it on an impulse. Now he was left trying to hide the truth of the matter. He wanted her to be his wife and, knowing that was going to happen, he didn't want to wait. It was just because of the baby, he told himself. He wanted his family settled. He didn't want his parents to be able to get in the way of this. He wasn't sure that they could stop him marrying, but he wouldn't put it past them to try.

'I don't want my parents interfering,' he said, wondering if that sounded as unconvincing as it felt. It didn't matter as long as they were clear about why they were telling themselves they were getting married.

And the reason didn't have anything to do with the night they had spent together. It

couldn't, because that was too complicated—
Hailey herself had said so. She was only marrying him out of obligation, and that was fine.
He'd come to terms with the fact already. It
was more than he had hoped for that *he* got to
choose his wife, rather than his parents or a
council of politicians. But that didn't make it a
love match. Hailey didn't love him. She didn't
even know him, and he'd spent enough of his
life giving love without it being returned to
expose himself to that sort of hurt again.

Whatever seeds of feelings he might have
for Hailey, he had to tamp them down and
remember that the choices that they made
should be based on what was right for their
child, not about their personal feelings.

'So we should move quickly if we want to
do this,' he said, wanting to move the conversation to practicalities.

'How quickly?'

'How do you feel about New Year's Eve?'

Hailey stopped walking abruptly. 'The New
Year's Eve that's on December the thirty-first,
two weeks from now?'

Gio nodded, sliding his hands into his
pockets and hoping that he hadn't given away
that his heart had stopped beating when she
had stopped walking. 'That's when it usually falls.'

'Two weeks is *not* enough time to arrange any wedding, Gio. Never mind a royal one.'

Gio held her gaze, trying to keep his expression free from emotion. 'The longer the planning goes on, the more complicated it'll get,' he countered. 'I want to keep things simple.'

There. They were back on track. That was a perfectly reasonable explanation for why he wanted to do this quickly, which had nothing to do with how he felt when he looked at Hailey or thought about the fact that she would soon be his wife.

But this wasn't a normal marriage. Pursuing this attraction would only make things exponentially more complicated. They had to concentrate on the most important aspect of their relationship, and that was as parents, not lovers. Hailey had made that much clear to him.

'I should be getting back,' Hailey said, glancing at the time on her phone. 'I've got a lot to organise if we're flying tonight.'

'Is that a yes to New Year's Eve?' Gio asked. He was well aware that it hadn't been but, as much as he didn't want to press her, he wanted to know that she was going through with this. That in two weeks he would be able to call her his wife.

'It's an *I'll think about it* to New Year's Eve,' Hailey told him with a slight frown.

'Then that will have to do, for now,' Gio conceded.

'It's all there is on offer right now.'

He nodded. 'I understand. I do. I won't pressure you.'

'You just want me to marry you and move halfway across the globe on half a day's notice.'

Hailey shook her head, because this wasn't Gio's fault. Now she was pregnant, all these complications were inevitable. That had been the risk she'd taken when she'd gone to bed with him that night. When she'd decided to keep the baby.

'I'm sorry,' she said, reaching out a hand to him in an attempt to find the ease between them that she'd taken for granted earlier. 'None of this is your fault. It's the universe that has made this complicated. You're just suggesting solutions—albeit somewhat radical ones.'

'I want to do the right thing,' Gio said with such earnestness that she had no choice but to believe him. No one proposed to a practical stranger for any other reason, especially when someone like him proposed to someone like her.

'I know. And I'm sure we are doing the right thing. Just let me get my head round it in my own time.'

As she threw clothes into her suitcase several hours later, she could only be thankful that she'd scheduled a break in her calendar following Ivy and Sebastian's big society wedding. There was nothing between now and January that her team couldn't manage without her, and by then she had to hope that she'd come up with a solution for how to run her business from Adria. She knew she could rely on Gracie to step in and help out with any crises. Except, that was, the crisis right in front of her—what to pack to meet your royal future in-laws, who were almost certainly going to hate you.

She could call Gracie and ask her advice, but she wasn't sure that she could talk to her again without spilling all her misgivings about the decisions that had led her here, and she couldn't be sure that if she did that she wouldn't change her mind and back out of the whole arrangement. For the sake of her baby, she had to hold her nerve, give her child the chance to know its family, its place in the world, in a way that had always been denied to her.

She hadn't thought that she'd ever have to do this again, stand over her suitcase and prepare to shift her life into someone else's family. But this was the price that she had to pay so that her baby never had to feel this. And she would pay it gladly for her child to have a better start in life than she'd had, so they could reach adulthood and find love on their own terms, secure in the knowledge that their parents had cherished them from the moment that they knew a baby existed.

In the end she went with practicality, throwing in thermals and knitwear, and some of the nicer outfits that she'd acquired for blending in at society weddings. The maternity jeans and leggings that she'd picked up last week, in anticipation of the day when leaving her top button undone was no longer a universal solution to what to wear.

She was never going to belong in Gio's family, but she'd try and hide that fact behind designer shirts if she could. She threw things in without looking, averting her eyes from the growing pile of clothes in the case. If she didn't look at it directly, it couldn't hurt her. Couldn't call back memories she'd long since buried—and she wanted it to stay that way. The knock at the door made her jump, and she wondered how long she'd been standing by her case, trying not to look at it.

She pulled the zip closed and answered the door, expecting to see Gio on the other side. But instead she was faced with a uniformed driver who gave her a professional nod at her look of surprise.

'I'm here to drive you to the airport, Ms Thomas,' he said. 'Can I help you with your bags?'

'It's just this one case,' she said, fighting down her disappointment that Gio had sent a driver for her rather than collecting her himself. It was foolish, she told herself. The man had asked her to marry him; she shouldn't be questioning his commitment to her. But there was a difference between commitment and…what? Personal interest? Was that what she wanted from him? They had both been very clear that they were only marrying for the sake of their baby. This arrangement was perfectly in line with what they had agreed.

She grabbed her bag herself, forcing a smile for the driver, and then surrendered it, throwing a handbag over her shoulder and pulling the door shut behind her. She turned the key in the lock, wondering when she would be back in her own space again. When she would be back in her own life rather than someone else's.

She shook her mind clear and followed the driver down the stairs and into the car. Scrolling through the news on her phone, she smiled when she stumbled across pictures of Ivy and Seb's wedding, seeing how beautifully Ivy's opulent vision of the day had materialised, and how proud she was of her team for their part in it. And she resisted the ever-present urge to open her messaging app to see whether she had missed a text from Gio, letting her know that he wouldn't be collecting her in person. He didn't owe her an explanation, and she figured she'd see him on the plane soon enough.

As the car passed through a gate into a private airport and then pulled up alongside a private jet, she decided there were going to be some things about living in Gio's world that she wouldn't exactly hate. She was glancing back down at her phone when the car drew to a halt and the door was opened for her. She looked up to see Gio standing at the top of the steps to the aircraft, and then he jogged down to the tarmac and held out a hand as she stepped from the car.

'Hailey,' he said, swooping in and kissing her on both cheeks. 'I'm sorry I couldn't collect you in person. There was something of a crisis and my father has been on the phone all afternoon and evening.'

She smiled, accepting his apology, and refusing to let her body react to the scent of him when he leaned in to kiss her. Following him up the steps, she lost the thread of what he was saying as she took in the luxurious interior of the cabin. Reclining leather chairs faced one another across the space, and a crystal decanter and glasses sat on a side table. Through an open door, she could see a separate cabin with a large bed, made up with acres of white cotton and monogrammed pillows. She looked away because she hadn't been in such close proximity to Gio and a bed since he'd got her pregnant, and that knowledge was doing something to her body that was very inconvenient, considering she was meant to be keeping this all about the baby and nothing else.

'It's fine,' she told him, bringing herself back to the present moment. 'I understand that you're busy. Is this crisis anything to do with…?' She raised her eyebrows, not wanting to speak out of turn in front of the cabin crew, knowing that people like Gio set store by confidentiality.

'No, that crisis won't be landing until tomorrow. Which is why I wanted this sorted today. I do try and keep Adria to one at a time.'

'Well, sorry to have made that more difficult for you,' she said, taking a seat when he gestured her towards one.

The cabin crew closed the door of the aircraft and then melted away with a discretion she assumed must be normal around the passengers of private jets.

'It's not like you got yourself pregnant,' he said with a smile. 'I should probably warn you, though, if things are a little…tense when we meet my family, it's nothing about you personally.'

'Well, that doesn't exactly fill me with confidence,' she said with a wry grin, trying to hide how horrifying the thought of being rejected by another family was for her. Fortunately, she interrupted herself with a yawn.

Gio smiled. 'You should take the cabin. Rest. I woke you at an unreasonable hour. You can try and get ahead of the jet lag.'

'Ha, in the life of a florist six a.m. is nothing, trust me. I'll hold out a little longer. You're the one who's still on European time. You should take it.'

'Take the only bed when my…' his pause was every bit as pregnant as she was '…fiancée,' Gio finished at last, and they both sat there with the word ringing in the air around them. That was truly going to take some getting used to. 'How about neither of us sleeps, and we have a drink and talk instead?' he suggested. 'What can I offer you?'

'Am I a terrible British cliché if I say tea?' Hailey asked.

Gio laughed. 'I should have thought of that before I brought you coffee this morning,' he said, calling over a crew member and ordering their drinks.

'Oh, no, that was definitely the right call,' Hailey said, taking a seat on one side of a highly polished side table. 'But I think we're out of New York airspace and that changes things. So,' she went on. 'Family politics. Give me the primer. I want to know what I'm letting myself in for.'

Gio sighed, sat opposite her and ran a hand through his hair.

'Is it that bad?' Hailey asked, looking at him with concern.

'Bad isn't the right word,' he told her as one of the cabin crew brought her tea on a silver tray, and a tumbler of some amber liquid for Gio. 'My family is…complicated,' he said, taking a sip and letting his eyes close for a second. 'I'm not just a son to them; I'm a junior partner in their firm. And that relationship always seems to be the one dictating how things are between us.'

'And that's why they think they have a right to choose who you marry?' Hailey asked, pouring her tea and stirring in milk.

'That's why they emphasise that I have responsibilities to consider before making big life decisions.'

'Which is why things are going to be frosty.'

He shrugged. 'I don't know. Maybe.'

She watched him carefully as his forehead creased and he took another sip of his drink. His head fell back against his seat and he closed his eyes. 'It's not too late to change your mind if you're having second thoughts,' she told him, more concerned in that moment about the tension that she saw on his face than their plans for the future.

'You're literally on the plane,' Gio said, opening his eyes and giving her a weak smile.

'I don't think that's legally binding,' Hailey said gently. 'We don't have to get married just because we shared a private jet.'

'Now you tell me.' She was relieved to see the corner of his lips quirk a little higher, but she was still waiting for one of those truly dazzling smiles of his. She wasn't sure when she had started to measure the mood of a room just by the breadth of his smile.

'I'm not having second thoughts,' Gio said, reaching for her hand, squeezing it and then leaving his palm covering hers. 'I know we are doing the right thing. But I also know that it's going to take some work on our part—on *my* part—to make my parents see it the same way.'

We're doing the right thing.

She repeated the words to herself as the plane taxied to the runway, trying to understand why they made the bottom of her stomach fall. Why they left her feeling so flat when it was the exact thing she was telling herself about why they were getting married. Fair enough… This whole thing would be more fairy tale if they were to fall for each other. But she wasn't in this for the fairy tale, no matter how her heart might give a little stutter at the thought of it. This relationship was about giving her child the best start in life. Nothing to do with how she had felt that night with Gio, or how her skin felt against his now. She drew her hand away.

'We *are* doing the right thing if it means you choosing the future that you want. We'll make sure your parents see tha—' Her last word was interrupted by another jaw-stretching yawn. When she opened her eyes, it was to find that Gio had fixed her with a stern look.

'You're going to bed,' he said, standing in front of her and offering his hand. She shouldn't take it. But the thought of those crisp white sheets and pillows—the idea of sleep—dragged her under. And if she was meeting the hostile in-laws tomorrow, she could at least do it looking more rested than she was sure she did right now.

'Okay. You're right,' she conceded. 'I had no idea growing a baby took so much energy. I mean, I'm not even really doing anything yet; it's barely more than a dot.'

She took Gio's hand and let him pull her up, neither of them moving when her change in position brought her body up against his. She craned her neck to look up at him and remembered how good that had felt. To have him above her and around her and inside her. How the real world had faded away out of respect for his—frankly perfect—frame. She cleared her throat, knowing that letting this moment draw out would cause nothing but trouble for them both.

The sound seemed to snap Gio back to his senses and he took a step back from her. 'I'll show you the cabin,' he said, and Hailey took the very grown-up decision to see absolutely no innuendo in that.

She followed him through the door, where he started pulling throw pillows off the bed and pulling back the sheets. 'The bathroom's just through there,' he said, indicating a door across the other side of the bed. She slid it open and found a small but immaculately appointed space, complete with shower, soft monogrammed towels and a counter stocked with luxury toiletries.

When she turned back, Gio was in the doorway to the cabin and the bed was turned down for her and looking more inviting than any horizontal surface with Prince Giovanni of Adria *beside* it instead of *in* it had any right to.

'Thanks,' she said, trying to keep her voice casual. 'Could you have someone wake me well before we land? I want the rest of that briefing before I meet your family.' She glanced back into the bathroom. 'And to try out that shower.'

Gio half smiled. 'Get some sleep, and do *not* worry about my parents. They're my problem.'

She held his gaze for a breath. 'I'm fairly sure that marriage makes things *our* problem. Otherwise, what's the point?'

Another almost-smile. What was a full one going to cost her, and could she remotely afford to pay? she wondered.

'Goodnight,' Gio said softly, and the intimacy of it sent a dangerous shiver up her spine. It was only because they were thirty thousand feet in the air in a glorified tin can that he was having this magnetic effect on her, making her question whether she had made the right call making their relationship all about the baby she was carrying, and not at all about the wild chemistry that had dragged them up to his suite that night and kept her pinned to his mattress—well, to various places, actually—until the sun had risen the next day.

As she slipped between the sheets, Gio started to turn away.

'Wait, where are you going to sleep?' she asked, suppressing a yawn.

'I'm fine,' he said, turning back towards her. 'Don't worry about me.'

'Too late for that.' She gave a dramatic sigh. 'Come on, you look exhausted. If I get to sleep, you get to sleep. The bed's plenty big enough and we're both too exhausted to do anything irresponsible.'

He stood looking at her in the doorway for long enough for her face to turn red and to wonder whether she'd just made a huge mistake. Well, she couldn't pretend she hadn't said it now. 'We're telling people that we're getting married,' she reminded him. 'We *are* getting married. People are going to find it strange if we act like polite strangers. And sleep in separate beds.'

'In the palace—'

'We're not in the palace. If there was another bed on this plane I'd be pushing you into it, but here we are. Okay, I'm going to sleep now. I'm leaving it up to you.'

She turned her back to the door, pressing her cheek against the cool cotton, hoping it would calm the hot flush of her face.

And then, above the noise of the aircraft engines, was the sound of leather-soled shoes on thick carpet. A pause as Gio stopped by the bed, and a dip and roll of the mattress as he slid in behind her.

A soft tapping brought Gio to wakefulness, and he pulled the warm body beside him close as he tried to work out where he was. Not his rooms at the palace. Not the hotel suite in New York either. Hailey gave a soft moan as she stirred, and it was as her eyes opened and her wide green gaze met his that he remembered.

'We'll be landing in fifteen minutes, Your Royal Highness,' the flight attendant called through the door.

Right. He had asked to be woken before they landed, back before he'd decided that caution and sleeping in a chair were over-rated and he'd accepted Hailey's invitation to sleep beside her.

This could, technically, just about, be considered 'beside her', he supposed. If one discounted the arm around her midriff and the way that he had used it to pull her tight when they were in that space between waking and sleeping. And the fact that he hadn't yet let her go.

'We should—' she started to say, and he sat upright in an instant, snapping back to reality, gathering the sheets around them. 'I'm going to…the bathroom,' Hailey said, her words faltering. 'Freshen up— No time to shower, but…' Her voice trailed off as she stood beside the bed.

'I'm sorry,' he said. 'I was asleep and I—'

She waved a hand, in a gesture he thought was supposed to look more casual than it actually did. 'It's nothing. Let's not mention it. I guess it's just something we're going to have to get used to.'

Get used to? he thought, as she slid closed

the door to the bathroom. There was no way he was ever going to get used to being so close to her and not being allowed to touch. It made so much more sense to think about their marriage in platonic terms. Something that they were doing for their baby, rather than examining the way that they felt about one another, or exploring the chemistry that kept pulling them together. There was enough going on without throwing sex into the mix. And there was no way he was going to risk falling for her when she was so clearly only doing this for the baby's sake.

If she accepted, their wedding would be two weeks away. That meant that he had two weeks to work out how he was meant to spend a lifetime alongside Hailey without falling for her.

Hailey emerged from the bathroom with her pink cheeks still damp from being splashed with water, and Gio clenched down on the lurch of his heart at the sight of her. He had to remember that this wasn't a fairy tale. He might have chosen Hailey himself, but this was no more a love match than if he'd accepted one of the suitable young women his parents had been pressing on him since he had turned twenty-one. It would be just as foolish believing Hailey could love him as it would have been to assume the same of any of that parade of convenient minor European princesses. The lines in their relationship could hardly be more blurred. But that didn't mean that he could let his emotions get confused. This was a sensible decision. The least bad course for his future was to spend it with a woman who he was already tied to for the rest of their lives. It wasn't the most generous assessment of their situation, but he had to remember that Hailey wasn't doing this because of her feelings about him.

Much like his parents, she was tolerating him. Tied by blood to one another's future. He already knew what would have happened if it wasn't for the biological glitch that had led to her pregnancy. She would have walked away from him—she *had* walked away from him—that morning in New York. No doubt she resented the fact that she was stuck with him, when she'd wanted to cut all ties—forget him as soon as that night was over. Or if she didn't now, she would eventually.

The plane touched down with barely a skitter on the runway of the private airfield, and he just had a chance to spot the anxious expression on Hailey's face.

'Hey,' he said, reaching out a hand and laying it on her arm. 'Are you okay?'

'Nervous,' she admitted, though the anxiety on her face was quickly replaced with fierce determination.

'It's still just us,' he said, suddenly feeling awkward and withdrawing his hand. 'The airfield is private, and I asked that no one meet us but the car. The family will be waiting for us at the palace.'

She let out a relieved breath. 'Okay. Stay of execution. How long until we meet them?'

'Twenty minutes?'

'Twenty minutes of real life left. Got it.'

'Sorry you have to spend it in the back of a car with me.'

She gave him a heated look. 'You know, I can think of worse ways…'

He grinned at her. They really had to stop flirting like this. Had to remember that this was no normal relationship. He had to stop this turning into a situation where he found himself wanting something that he knew he could never properly have.

His own parents had never loved him. He'd known a long time ago not to expect love in a royal family. He would settle for someone who liked him. And, to do that, he had to manage his expectations and make sure he didn't give away more of himself than he was ever going to get back in return.

The back seat of the car saw absolutely no action besides Hailey carefully knitting her fingers together over and over, until he reached out and laid his palm over them, stroking the back of her hand with his thumb. 'I promise it'll be okay,' he told her, wishing his words alone would be enough to soothe the worried lines from her forehead.

She gave him a weak smile. 'You've changed your tune.'

'I never said it wouldn't be okay. It might get a little…awkward, at first. I grant you that. But it will all be okay in the end. I promise.'

She snorted lightly. '*In the end…* You do realise that leaves quite a lot of scope for how long things can be "awkward", as you put it. Are we talking ten days or ten years for this *in the end*? Roughly speaking.'

'Roughly speaking? I can't be sure.'

He stepped through the door of the palace, acknowledging the doorman with a nod, and laced his fingers through Hailey's as they headed towards his parents' rooms. He had no doubt that his parents would be waiting for him there.

The ceiling soared twenty feet above their heads, greenery was wreathed around every horizonal surface and quite a few vertical ones too. A fire roared in the grate, surrounded by a collection of furniture that was worn in the very expensive way that only the truly wealthy managed to achieve. Gio had stiffened beside her, and his tight grip on her fingers tugged at something in her heart. Because she was the one who was about to come face to face with her royal future in-laws, who she was fairly sure were going to hate her. And yet he—Crown Prince Giovanni of Adria, their cherished son and heir—was the one who was nervous.

'Mother,' Gio said as they walked into the grand reception room, and Hailey stood rooted to the spot, waiting for the drama to begin.

'Giovanni, you're home,' said his mother, Queen Lucia. An elegant woman dressed all in black, she sat with ankles crossed and tucked demurely beneath her, her hands folded tightly in her lap. 'You've brought a guest,' she added, looking pointedly at Hailey in a way that made her wish she wasn't currently encased in a thick parka.

Hailey's heart stuttered and she forced herself not to turn to look questioningly at Gio. He hadn't *told* them she was coming?

The squeeze of Gio's hand stopped the

words in her throat. He hadn't given her any reason not to trust him. If he hadn't told his parents she was coming, she was sure that he must have had his reasons.

Queen Lucia rose to stand and stalked towards them at such a glacial pace that it had to be a deliberate power move. In sleek black cigarette pants and a fitted sweater, her hair caught up in a chignon that would put any Parisian coiffeur to shame, she barely looked old enough to be Gio's mother. When she reached them, Gio stepped forward and kissed his mother on both cheeks.

'Mamma,' he said, 'may I present Ms Hailey Thomas?'

Hailey fought the sudden urge to curtsey.

'How do you do,' the older woman said, her eyes barely leaving Gio's long enough to flicker disapprovingly over Hailey.

'How do you do, Your Majesty,' Hailey replied. Thanks for *that*, *Debrett's* etiquette section, she thought, seeing a flicker of approval on the Queen's face. Well, she'd got one thing right, at least. But they'd see soon enough how far that approval stretched when she found out about the baby. And the engagement.

'You should have let us know that you were

bringing a friend,' the Queen admonished her son. 'I shall have to speak to the housekeeper.'

'There's no need. Hailey will share my room.' So much for that talk about separate rooms, Hailey thought, trying not to let her surprise show on her face.

The Queen's eyes, however, widened just a fraction before she regained that tiny fraction of composure.

'Of course, if you wish. Come, sit by the fire,' she said, gesturing formally as a maid came to relieve them of coats and their luggage disappeared upstairs.

'Is Father here?' Gio asked as he took a seat on a stiff-backed sofa and pulled Hailey down beside him with their linked hands. His fingers were still tightly threaded between hers, and she couldn't help the feeling that he was holding on for dear life.

As he spoke, King Leonardo emerged through a doorway in the corner of the great hall. Gio's back stiffened further—something that Hailey hadn't thought was possible—and he made as if to stand until his father waved his hand.

'No need to get up, son. I heard you arrive.'

'Father,' Gio said, as the King took a seat opposite.

'Have you introduced your guest?'

They went through the formalities, Gio's voice becoming more strained the longer that they sat there.

'Well, Giovanni. You said on the phone that you needed to speak to us in person.' The royal couple both shot Hailey a questioning look. 'I suggest you tell us what this is about so that we can deal with whatever needs dealing with.'

It didn't take a genius to work out that *she* was what needed dealing with in this situation, and if Gio's parents hadn't guessed the full extent of the trouble, they had to be at least halfway there.

Gio fixed his eyes on his father, gripped Hailey's hand a little tighter and spoke with a tense jaw.

'Hailey and I are expecting a baby,' he said without a hint of emotion in his voice. 'We're also engaged. The wedding will take place on New Year's Eve. I would like it if you could congratulate us.'

The four of them sat in silence, the hoped-for congratulations conspicuously absent. The Queen cleared her throat as the King's face grew red.

'Are you asking for our permission or our blessing?' Queen Lucia asked eventually.

'Neither,' Gio replied, his voice as cold as

his mother's. 'I'm informing you of our plans. I'm an adult—I don't need your permission to marry.'

'You're the Crown Prince of Adria,' his father countered.

Hailey had to fight the urge to roll her eyes. Did he think that Gio could possibly have forgotten that fact? But it didn't stop him droning on.

'You have responsibilities. Your marriage is a question for me, your mother and our advisors. Do you have any idea how difficult this is going to be to undo? Who else knows about this?'

Hailey couldn't help but notice it was the same question Gio had asked her when she had told him that she was pregnant, and wondered whether Gio had realised it too.

'I don't think you understand, Father,' Gio said, and she could hear in his voice how much this steady control was costing him. 'Our wedding will take place in two weeks' time. Our baby will be born in the summer. I'm informing you as a courtesy only because this is happening whether you like it or not.'

That 'or not' was somewhat redundant, wasn't it? Hailey thought. They couldn't have been any clearer that they absolutely did *not* like this.

'Are you sure she's pregnant?' Queen Lucia asked, speaking for the first time since Gio had shared their news, and staring at her son as if Hailey wasn't sitting right there in front of her. 'And that the baby is yours?'

'I'm sure. We're delighted,' Gio replied, honestly sounding nothing of the sort, but she appreciated the gesture nonetheless.

'Then I have nothing more to say to you,' Queen Lucia said, standing and brushing down her already immaculate trousers. She had left the room before Hailey had a chance to close her mouth. She glanced across at Gio to see how he had taken her rudeness and found his face a blank indifferent mask.

Gio's father followed his wife out of the room, leaving the two of them sitting beside the fire in a space that could grace any Christmas card, with its looping pine boughs, bright silver bells and sprigs of berries. And yet the mood was decidedly more frosty than festive.

'Well, that went well,' Hailey said with an ironic smile, giving Gio's hand a squeeze before dropping it—no need to keep up the pretence that they were in love with one another now they didn't have an audience.

Gio let his head tip back against the back of the chair and rubbed a hand over his face.

'I'm so sorry I subjected you to that,' he said, muffled slightly by the hand that still half blocked his face.

'No,' Hailey said gently. 'I'm sorry that they spoke to you like that. Are you okay?'

'Yes.' Gio emerged from behind his hand. 'I'm fine. That's almost exactly how I expected it to go.'

'Then I'm sorry for that too,' she said. She'd spent her life longing for a family, and had never considered that you could be just as lonely in the heart of one as you could be on the outside looking in.

'What happens next?' she asked. 'Do we just leave things like that?'

'Next, we arrange the wedding,' Gio said, sitting forward and resting his elbows on his knees.

'Without their blessing?'

He shrugged. 'I have my own office. They'll take care of the arrangements.'

'That's not what I meant,' Hailey said.

Gio let out a breath. 'I know it's not. But I'm not going to change how they feel. We make our plans and we make the best of it.'

'"We make the best of it"?' she repeated. 'I'm not sure a happy marriage has ever followed those words.'

He fixed her with a piercing look. 'A happy

marriage has never been an option for me. Not the way that you mean.'

'Then why are we doing this?' she asked, trying to protect herself from the hurt that threatened at his words.

'For the baby,' Gio said, his eyes narrowed slightly. 'I thought that's what we were doing.'

'Yes. When I thought that was what you wanted. That it would make you happy, even if not in the hearts and flowers way some people might want.'

'You don't want hearts and flowers?' Gio asked.

Hailey rolled her eyes. As if the answer to that wasn't obvious. 'I agreed to this, didn't I?'

'I'm sorry,' Gio said, shaking his head. 'I know it's not enough.'

She reached for his hand. 'It's not too late to change your mind,' she told him again, though each time she said it, it felt less and less true.

'I could say the same to you,' Gio replied, squeezing her fingers.

She laid his hand on her belly and looked up at him. 'It's too late for me. I want this baby to know its family. To belong. I have to make it work.'

'Even though it's *this* family?'

'You don't get to choose your family.'

'Never was a truer word spoken,' Gio said, turning up the corner of his mouth, but the strain around his eyes prevented it from turning into a real smile. She wondered if she would see the real one again.

'I don't want to change my mind,' he said. 'I want you. This. I want *us* to be a family.'

'Then you'd better start making some calls. New Year's Eve is only a fortnight away.'

Gio's parents didn't join them for dinner, and as the evening wore on it became apparent that they weren't going to join them at all. Hailey sat and watched as Gio grew tenser and tenser, sipping at a single glass of whisky, his knuckles white on the cut crystal.

'If they're going to snub us, we might as well call it a night,' Gio said eventually, after they'd passed the evening in a formal drawing room in silence, watching the fire burn low.

'Fine by me,' Hailey said, interrupting herself with a huge yawn. 'This baby hasn't got the jet lag message. I could definitely sleep.'

'Good.' Gio stood and reached out a hand to help her up. 'I'll show you our rooms.' He kept hold of her hand as they climbed the stairs. The words were on her lips to tell him it wasn't a good idea to share a room. But she remembered the look on his face when his parents had let him know what they felt about their first grandchild and, whether it was a good idea or not, she didn't want to leave him alone with whatever thoughts were causing that pained expression.

Gio opened a door into a comfortably furnished sitting room, the walls covered with an elegantly mismatched collection of bookshelves and one wall with windows out onto the snow-covered gardens. Through an open door she could see a bedroom beyond, and through another a small kitchen. Stepping through into the bedroom, she sighed with satisfaction. It was lit by flickering firelight, the walls were panelled in warm old wood and the floor was scattered with thick, plush rugs. The four-poster bed was hung with tapestried curtains and piled high with embroidered, tasselled cushions in warm colours.

'You take the bed,' Gio said, pulling cushions from it and tossing them onto the antique-looking sofa on one side of the open fire.

'Not this again,' Hailey said, pulling open the wardrobe and finding her clothes pressed and hanging inside.

'The rest of your things will be in the drawers,' Gio said, clearly spotting her wide-eyed awareness that her clothes had been magically unpacked and pressed.

'We're going to be married in a fortnight. We need to learn to sleep in the same bed. I'm going to be wearing at least three layers of flannel and I think I can trust myself,' Hailey said.

'Who said it was you I was worried about?'

Gio looked her straight in the eye for so long that she felt her cheeks warm.

'Come on, Gio, don't tease. We're being sensible about this.'

'I'm sorry. Okay, we'll share for now. But I'm arranging for you to have your own rooms in case you change your mind. I shouldn't have told my parents we would share without asking you first. And you don't have to worry. It's perfectly usual for royal couples to have separate chambers.'

'All those generations of unhappy marriages,' she mused.

'I don't want to be one of them,' Gio said, sitting on the edge of the bed and gesturing for Hailey to sit beside him. She perched up on the mattress, and when it gave way beneath her, pitching her closer to Gio, she didn't fight it and let the side of her body rest against his.

'I know that we wouldn't be doing this if

it wasn't for the baby. But I want to try, Hailey. I want to try and be happier than my parents are. There was something between us, that night. Wasn't there? And I'm not talking about the sex, I'm talking about us. Is that enough to base a marriage on?'

'It's enough to be a start, at least,' she said. 'And I want to try too. Let's try and build a friendship. By being there for one another. Let's see where that takes us.'

She let her head come to rest on his shoulder. 'Okay, but I'm still wearing the flannel.'

He laughed against her cheek. 'I'm all out of flannel.'

'Well, find something to sleep in because I want this friends thing to work, and I'm only human.'

'I didn't realise I was so irresistible.'

She looked up at him with a grin. 'Yes, you did. You absolutely did. And I'm not going to massage your ego any further.' She got up from the bed and found her pyjamas in a drawer of the enormous bureau.

In the bathroom, she removed her makeup and splashed cold water on her cheeks, hoping it would cool the hot pink flush she could see in the mirror. This was perfectly fine. This was sharing an enormous bed with someone who was going to be a friend. The fact that their relationship had started with a fiercely hot one-night stand didn't have to come into it.

When she got back into the bedroom, the sheets were turned down and the lamps by the bed were lit. The curtains were all closed against the cold night and the overhead light was off, bathing the whole room in a warm orange glow.

She climbed into bed with her pyjamas buttoned to the neck, and was immediately swallowed up by the soft mattress and the heavy layers of blankets and quilts.

Gio emerged in the doorway of the bathroom and Hailey turned her head on the cold pillow, wondering if the circulation in her face was ever going to feel normal again. Was she really signing up for a lifetime of this? she asked herself. Of being so distracted by her husband—her *husband*—that she could barely look him straight in the eye?

It would fade, she promised herself. This feeling. This need for him. It was pure lust, and if they ignored it for long enough it would fade. When that happened, they would work out some friendly arrangement so that they didn't spend the rest of their lives celibate. Maybe they'd stay married in name only, with a discreet arrangement for their future love lives.

Except…except she couldn't see that happening. Not for her, at least. She simply couldn't imagine a life with Gio in it where she wanted someone else more than she wanted him.

So perhaps, in time, when the intensity of their first meeting had fully faded, they'd fall into bed again in a safe, companionable, married sort of way that wouldn't have the power to hurt her.

She felt Gio slip into the bed beside her and turned to look at him, one hand tucked under her cheek, the other under her pillow. 'Managing to resist so far?' he asked, a curve to one side of his lips as he mirrored her body language, his cheek to the pillow, hands tucked beneath them. And she realised how impossible it was to imagine feeling 'companionable' about him.

'The whisky breath is helping,' she said, knowing that it would make him laugh.

'I say,' he objected, nudging her knee with his. 'I brushed. And flossed.'

'Such a good boy,' she said mockingly. 'So wholesome.' Though the words died in her mouth because they both knew he was nothing of the sort.

'It's nice, having you here,' Gio said out of nowhere, and that blush was back on her cheeks.

'I like it too,' Hailey admitted. That was safe, surely. They were going to be married by the end of the month. It was safe to say that she liked being here. It didn't say anything that she hadn't already implied by accepting his proposal. Just so long as she didn't lose sight of the fact that liking it here didn't mean that she got to stay. Didn't mean that she'd been accepted. One day, when their baby was settled and in no doubt about where they belonged, she and Gio would move on. She was just the vessel for the baby's place in this family. She would never belong. Not properly. And that was fine. She'd spent her whole life on the periphery of families she didn't quite belong to. She had plenty of practice at not letting that hurt her. As long as she remembered what this was. As long as she remembered that her place here was only temporary and that Gio and his family couldn't hurt her if she remembered that fact, then she would be fine.

'Where did you go?' Gio asked, and when she looked across at him she found his brow slightly furrowed.

'Just thinking,' she said, her voice quiet in the scant inches between them.

'About?' Gio prompted.

She sighed. Where could she start?

'Nothing important,' she lied. 'Just wondering where all this will end up. The wedding. Then the baby. Then parenting. And then what? What comes next?'

'Whatever we choose,' Gio said, as if it would all be as simple as that. Perhaps it would. Perhaps, one day, he would simply choose someone who wasn't her and she would go back to her safe old life in New York. Become a peripheral part of a royal family. Third wheel to a more prestigious circle than her childhood foster families, but ultimately no more wanted than she had been then.

'Try and get some sleep,' Gio said, pressing his lips to her forehead. 'Tomorrow's going to be a busy one, and our baby could change its mind about the jet lag.'

CHAPTER SEVEN

GIO WATCHED AS Hailey's eyes closed, watched on in wonder as sleep dragged her under as easily as she drew breath. Despite the tiredness he could feel in his bones, the sleep he would have welcomed with open arms never came. He would have liked to chalk it up to the change of time zones, and yet he knew that would be a lie.

It was the fact that he was lying next to the woman he'd barely been able to stop thinking about since the night that they had spent together, knowing that his baby was growing inside her. That in two weeks he would call her his wife. And at some point after that they would have to work out what being married would actually mean for them. Not love, of course. He knew better than to expect that to grow out of what was an arrangement rather than a relationship. But friendship, perhaps. Respect. Companionship. That could be enough, he told himself.

He couldn't even face the question of where that would leave their physical relationship. Would Hailey want that, one day? he couldn't help but wonder. He knew she was attracted to him. And they'd proved well beyond doubt already how good it was between them.

How complicated could it be, sleeping with his wife? Endlessly complicated, he acknowledged, if he had to stop himself from falling for her. He wasn't sure he could trust himself to do that.

He woke the way he had finally fallen asleep, his nose mere inches away from Hailey's, her hands still tucked beneath her cheek, as if she'd moved not an inch since he'd finally closed his eyes. He turned away from her slowly, reaching for his phone to check the time and then sliding out of the bed, deciding to leave her to sleep. She still looked tired, the shadows beneath her eyes not quite faded. And even if it weren't for that, he didn't want her to have to hear what he was sure his parents would have to say to him.

He found them at the table in the formal dining room, sitting opposite one another in silence, each of them sipping coffee and reading a newspaper. His mother looked up from hers as he stepped into the room, before placing it carefully beside her plate.

'Are you alone?' she asked.

'Yes,' Gio said. 'I didn't want to wake Hailey.'

'Good. Because we should talk before this goes any further.'

Gio nodded and took a seat beside his father. There was no point trying to stop them saying their piece. Perhaps once they'd done so, and they'd aired their concerns, they'd be able to leave him alone, knowing that they had at least tried.

'I know you think you're doing the honourable thing in marrying the girl,' his mother said. 'And I can respect that. But I think what would be best for the whole family is if she simply went back to America. If the child is born out of wedlock it won't impact the succession, and I'm sure we'll be able to find you a more suitable bride who will be understanding about these things. You could still take care of them financially, of course.'

'"The girl"? "The child"?' Gio said, anger making his words sharp. 'That's *my* child you're talking about, and the woman *I'm* going to marry. If they go back to America, then so do I.'

'You're being ridiculous, Giovanni,' his

mother said dismissively, gesturing to a footman to pour her another cup of coffee. 'The
Crown Prince of Adria cannot simply move to
another country. You need to be here, where
you can get to know your people and they can
get to know you.'

'Then I won't be Crown Prince anymore,'
Gio said, looking his mother straight in the
eye, his voice perfectly calm now. 'If you're
going to make me, then I choose them. A normal life. A normal family.'

'Now you're being rash,' his mother said,
stirring cream into her coffee and looking at
him over the rim as she took a sip.

'You're forcing me to be. I'm going to make
this very clear for you. You welcome Hailey.
You make sure the whole world sees that you
are delighted for us. For your first grandchild.
Or I'm leaving. It's as simple as that.'

They both stared at him in silence as he
reached for the coffee pot and poured himself
a cup with a rock-steady hand. He sat, sipped
his coffee. Waited.

He felt no pressure because, quite honestly,
he couldn't care less what they said. If anything, it would be a relief if they turned him
away and never wanted to see him again. But
he didn't have to think too hard to know that
was never going to happen. He was their only

child, the sole heir to the kingdom, and they wouldn't risk the succession over his choice of wife. Over the mother of his child.

His father broke first. Taking a sip of his coffee, he fixed him with a seemingly casual look over the rim of his cup. 'If she's your choice, then of course you have our support, son.'

Of course. Classic parental move. To make him feel as if he were the one who had caused the conflict rather than them.

'Mamma?'

She looked up at him, feigning surprise. 'Of course we'll support you,' she said with a raised eyebrow. 'If you're certain you're not making a mistake.'

And that was the best he could hope for, he supposed, in terms of parental support. Really, he couldn't have asked for clearer proof that he was making the right decision, that he owed it to himself, and to Hailey and their baby, to make his own family in his own way.

'Wonderful,' he told them, his voice heavy with sarcasm. 'We'll begin making plans today.'

'We'll wait to hear from your office what is expected of us then,' his mother said, reaching for her newspaper again, and he knew he was dismissed. He plucked a croissant from the basket at the centre of the table, wrapped it in a heavy linen napkin and left the room, coffee in hand.

'Is that for me?' Hailey asked, pushing herself up on her elbows as Gio walked into the room, and he passed the croissant over without hesitation.

'It is. I can have something else sent up if you want.'

'No,' Hailey said, sitting up properly now and taking the pastry from him, suddenly realising she was famished. 'This is perfect. Is the coffee for me too?'

He passed over the cup. 'As long as you don't mind sharing.'

'We've shared more.' She smiled. 'Sorry, that was crude.'

But Gio grinned as he sat on the side of the bed. 'Don't apologise on my account. I rather liked the things we shared.'

She grinned at him over their shared cup of coffee.

'Did you talk to your parents again?' she asked, feeling the carbs and coffee hit her system, restoring some sense of normality.

'How did you know?'

'You have a look.' Lines on his forehead,

tense muscles in his jaw, ramrod-straight spine. 'How did it go?' she asked.

'As well as one could have hoped,' Gio said, and she wondered whether he really thought that she would fall for that kind of polite evasion.

'Terrible, then?'

Gio nodded. 'I threatened to renounce my title and leave the country. That sorted things out.'

Hailey froze, her cup halfway to her lips. He couldn't seriously have threatened to do that for her. For the baby, she corrected herself. 'You didn't,' she said.

'Actually, I did.' For the first time the muscle in Gio's jaw eased slightly.

'Why would you do that?'

'Because I don't want to be part of a family that doesn't welcome my wife and child.'

Well, didn't that just hit her right in the centre of the chest? Because perhaps it was the two of them, standing on the edge of this family, not quite accepted at the centre.

'And what did they say?' she asked.

'That I was being rash.'

She snorted. 'Well, they weren't entirely wrong.'

'I meant it, though,' Gio said, reaching for her hand, his face earnest. 'I'll move to New

York, if that's what you want. If you want a normal life for this baby. My family—it's… far from ideal.'

'But it's your family,' she said. 'And our baby's too. I don't want to take them away from the place where they belong.' Was that really what was most important, she had to ask, even if it wasn't where Gio wanted to be? But she had to try—belonging to a family was what she'd wanted her whole life, and she couldn't just decide for her baby that they wouldn't have that—even if it hurt Gio.

'The baby belongs with your family too,' Gio said, which was her cue, she supposed, to confess to her lack of one.

'Ah, well,' she said, trying to keep her voice casual. 'I don't really have a family.'

'I'm sorry,' Gio said, reaching for her hand. 'Do you want to talk about it?'

'There's not really much to talk about. But I suppose I should tell you the whole story, because we'll have to think about how to handle the press. I don't know my biological parents—they gave me up for adoption when I was a baby. After that there were children's homes and foster families. I was adopted as an older child, and they were nice people, but it was too late for them to feel like *my* family.'

'I'm sorry,' Gio said earnestly. 'That sounds...
lonely.'

Hailey shrugged. 'It is what it is. But I don't
want our baby to be...rootless, like I am.'

'And that's why you agreed to the marriage,' Gio said, realisation clearly dawning.

'I don't want you cutting off your family
just because they don't like me,' she said with
a sudden pang of guilt.

Gio shook his head. 'It's not that they don't
like you. They don't know you. They just
have their own ideas for my future, and they
think they should be the ones making decisions for me.'

'I don't care if they like me. I wouldn't expect them to in the circumstances.'

'If I walked away from people who don't
support me it wouldn't be the same thing. I
don't want you to worry about me.'

'But I do.' She reached out a hand and
stilled him with her palm on his cheek. 'I do
care, Gio.'

He forced a smile. 'Of course you do. For
the baby's sake. I do understand, you know.'

'No, you don't. I care for your sake. I don't
like seeing you hurt.'

And she didn't want to think too hard about
why that was. But she'd had years to accept
that her parents had hurt her. The wound

was healed—scarred, and angry, but no longer open. Gio's wounds were fresh and she couldn't bear to see how it was hurting him.

He turned his face into her palm until his lips brushed the heel of her hand. Then, with a sigh, he pulled away, wrapped his fingers around hers and let their joined hands fall to the blankets.

'I'm not hurt. And you don't have to protect me.'

She could accept the second half of that declaration. And he might be able to hide his hurt from himself, but she could see it clear as day. But if he wasn't ready to talk about it, she didn't have any choice but to accept that.

'What time is it?' she asked, feeling a strong need to change the subject.

'Nearly ten,' Gio replied, looking relieved. 'I have a meeting with my chamberlain in an hour to start making arrangements for the wedding. In the meantime, what would you like to do—a tour of the palace? A more substantial breakfast? A longer lie-in?'

'How about another cup of coffee and a tour?'

'Perfect. I'll have a tray sent up and let you get dressed. Just come through when you're ready.'

'Gio…' she said as he was about to turn

away. He raised an eyebrow. She looked him up and down—well-pressed shirt and trousers. His hair neater than she'd ever seen it. 'What does one wear to tour a palace?'

He smiled. 'Whatever you're comfortable in will be perfect.'

She nodded, not sure if she should say what she was thinking. That she couldn't care less whether she was wearing the right thing in the eyes of his parents, but he so obviously cared about their good opinion and she didn't want to add to his distress. In the end, she pulled out a pair of black jeans and the cashmere sweater she'd 'borrowed' after their night together. Perhaps she'd feel a little more as if she belonged here. In the closet she found that her black leather boots had been cleaned and polished and she pulled them on.

When she left the bedroom Gio was waiting for her in the living room of their apartment. He smiled at the sight of her, and she knew that he recognised his sweater but didn't say anything. He just poured her a cup of coffee from the silver tray that had appeared on the coffee table and held it out to her. His expression was carefully guarded, the result, she was sure, of her gentle probing into his feelings about his parents. So she kept their conversation on safer ground as they toured the palace, asking questions about the portraits hanging along the walls in their gilt frames. Gently teasing him about why a palace required a Crystal Ballroom *and* a Gold Ballroom, and how one decided which of one's ballrooms to use when one was throwing a ball. As Gio told her the stories of his forebears in the palace, she watched his shoulders drop, his gait loosen and the hint of a smile return to his mouth.

'You don't want a ballroom for our wedding?' Gio asked. 'You can choose Crystal or Gold. Whatever your heart desires, Princess.'

'I thought you wanted to keep things simple,' Hailey said with a startled laugh.

'I do,' Gio replied. 'But I realise I never actually asked if that's what you want, which was unforgivable of me. If you want a ballroom, of course you can have a ballroom.'

She shook her head. 'Small and simple suits me just fine. I'd feel a little awkward not filling my half of a ballroom.'

'I'm sorry; I didn't think,' Gio said. 'But if there's anyone you would like to invite, you should. I know it's short notice, but one of the benefits of marrying into my family is that we are good with the logistics of flying people around.'

She shook her head. 'Really, there's only

Gracie, and I couldn't ask her to disrupt her holiday plans.'

Gio frowned at her. 'I don't know. I got the feeling that she would disrupt just about anything if you asked her to.'

'Which is why I'm careful about what I ask for. I wouldn't want to put her out.'

Gio looked at her long enough that she shifted in her boots, until she rolled her eyes, breaking their eye contact and turning away from him. 'Then let's go look at the morning room. It's beautiful with the low sun at this time of year. I think you'll like it.'

He led her through a series of opulent chambers, the names and functions of which she couldn't hope to guess at, until Gio opened the door to a small room with walls lined in cream silk, the sun slanting in low through windows that reached from the distant ceiling to the tops of the baseboards.

A small cluster of silk-upholstered chairs was arranged around a roaring fire and a pretty writing bureau faced the windows out onto the snow-covered formal gardens.

'What do you think?' Gio asked, hands clasped behind his back.

'I think it's beautiful,' Hailey said. Because what other word could she use to describe such a fairy tale location?

'How many people will be attending?' she asked, suddenly realising she had no idea what a 'small' royal wedding looked like.

'As many or as few as we want,' Gio said. 'Though my parents will expect certain dignitaries to be on the guest list. I have an inconvenient number of cousins. I'll keep it as small as I can, but it would make life easier if we give in on a few of the more senior names.'

'If it makes things easier with your parents, then of course do what you have to do.'

He smiled and nodded. 'I have friends too, from school and university, that I'd like to invite. But the timing will make it awkward so hopefully a lot of them won't be able to make it. I quite like the idea that this is something for us. Not some grand performance.'

'I agree. And in the circumstances... I moved around a lot as a child and didn't make any friendships that survived my move to New York. Things with my adoptive parents are... This is rather *a lot* to have to explain to them. Never mind expecting them to come here and be a part of this circus. I know I should tell them, but I honestly don't know...'

She turned to look out of the window and her shoulder bumped against Gio's side. She should move away from him, but the feel of him beside her was comforting and she would take whatever reassurance she could get at the moment.

'I can't wait to see these gardens in the summer,' she said. 'They must be spectacular.'

'Remind me to introduce you to the head gardener,' Gio said, leaning back into her just a fraction. 'I'm sure you two would have a lot to talk about.'

'I'd like that,' Hailey said, thinking. It was only just starting to sink in how much she had left behind in New York, with no idea if she was ever going back.

She had built her business with her own cold, red, chapped hands. Bleaching buckets in Gracie's shop at five in the morning. Putting in eighteen-hour days in the run-up to weddings, conditioning flowers and putting in the extra effort to deliver anything her clients demanded. Eventually, she'd outgrown Gracie's business and, with her friend's support and the growing reputation of her fine art style, had branched out on her own, building her client list for high-profile events, with her own team of assistants, hand-picked and trained by her and Gracie until they worked like a well-planned, well-executed machine.

Sure, they would be able to handle the events she'd already designed without her. The designs for the next two months were already signed off with the clients. She could absolutely trust her team to bring them to life.

God knew she could do with a break from her endlessly freezing cold workshop, snipping stems and sweeping away the forest carpet of foliage that gathered as they trimmed away leaves.

But the designs? She had never considered giving that up. When she had met Gracie, discovered the art she could create, the emotions she could evoke with her floral installations, she had finally found her place. She had built her whole adult life, her whole adult identity, around her love of art, her job and her business. Without those, who was she? Was she the lost, rootless girl she had been when she'd landed in the United States for the first time?

She remembered the lonely young woman she had been back then and shivered.

'Are you cold?' Gio asked, pulling her into his side with an arm around her shoulder, but she shook her head and stepped away from him.

'Just wondering how my team are getting on without me. I have a lot of decisions to make about what to do with the business. I don't see how I can continue to run it if I'm living here.'

'I'm sorry. I hate how much you're having to give up to be here.'

'You don't need to apologise,' she told him. 'Give me enough credit to know that I can make my own choices. I want to be here. I just don't know enough about what my life will be like here to know if I can run a business. I've got no contacts. No clients. No suppliers.'

'You have talent and experience, wherever you decide to use it. And a royal household at your disposal.'

'And while I'm grateful for that, I'm not sure that I want my business relying on inherited privilege.'

Gio crossed his arms and faced her. 'Like my life is? Like our child's life will be?'

'I don't know, Gio! I want to be here. I want to be with you! I just don't know how any of this works in practice. I'm going to be a princess, for goodness' sake. I don't know *how* to be a princess.'

'You want to be with me?' Gio said, taking a step towards her so that she had to crane her neck to look up at his face, and her whole body hummed with awareness of how close he was. But she had to concentrate on what they were talking about here.

'For God's sake, Gio. That's the part of this you hear? This whole situation is so confusing. I have no idea what my life is going to look like a month from now. And it's making me want to hold onto those things that I *do* know extra hard. And that's one of them. I don't know where that leaves us.'

Gio's body language relaxed and he turned back towards the window.

'It leaves us with the things we can control now,' he said gently, and she took solace from the calm competence in his voice. 'Which right now is the wedding, where we want to spend Christmas and keeping you well and the baby well. Would you like to meet with the palace physician?'

'Do we have a choice over where we spend Christmas?' she asked.

'If we want to,' he told her. 'We have a ski lodge up in the mountains. We could escape, just the two of us. Leave all the rigmarole of the royal stuff behind.'

God, that was tempting. Dangerous, but so very, very tempting. But a sure-fire way of pissing off the in-laws and guaranteeing tension in their future relationship. 'That isn't exactly going to endear me to your family,' she told him 'Stealing you away for my first Christmas here.'

'I don't care what they think,' he said with a shrug.

'Well, I do,' she said. She didn't have the luxury of not caring, like he did. 'I'm going to have to live with their opinion of me, and it's low enough as it is. I don't want you shielding me from them.'

'Then we'll spend Christmas here,' he said. 'But trust me. Give it a week and you'll be begging me for a break.'

CHAPTER EIGHT

THE TEN DAYS until Christmas had stretched before her like an eternity, making her wonder how she was going to fill the time. For a 'small' wedding with only a handful of guests, it seemed to require just as much planning as the largest society wedding. And as much as she and Gio had told his parents and their staff that they didn't need to sign off on every detail, still the questions kept coming. About menus, vows, music, candles. The only area where Hailey truly had an opinion was, of course, the flowers.

She sat with the head gardener and the palace florist, talking about what was in season locally, what was flowering in the greenhouses, what displays had already been planned for the holidays and could be adapted for a wedding.

She walked in the forest with the groundskeepers, pointing out foliage for garlands to be strung, wound and arranged around the morning room where the ceremony would take place and the stairs where the Queen was insisting that they had formal photographs taken. They had at least managed to draw the line at a press conference on the wedding day itself. Instead they had promised official engagement photographs in exchange for an embargo on the news until Christmas Eve and the press keeping their distance from the wedding itself.

She had a video conference with her ob-gyn in New York and a local specialist she and Gio had chosen, to ensure her continuity of care whether they were in Adria or New York.

She now stood looking at the rail of dresses that Gio's private secretary had sent over for approval. It was Christmas Eve, snowing, below freezing outdoors, which meant it was barely above that temperature in the vast formal rooms of the palace. How was she meant to choose what to wear? This was more than just what she liked and what was comfortable. The dress she chose today would be photographed and shared around the world in an instant. This outfit was going to be all that people knew about her. If she chose a designer outfit, would she look out of touch?

If she went high street, was she going to be the commoner who was dragging the royal family and the whole of Adria into the gutter she'd emerged from?

She flicked through the rail: navy trouser suit, emerald shift dress, a deep ruby wrap dress cut on the bias, with a cascade of pleats to the front. Well, that would solve the baby bump issue, she supposed, which had suddenly decided to make itself known on the morning of the photoshoot. She checked the notes that Gio's chamberlain had provided with each outfit, with the details about where each item had come from.

This one was from an up-and-coming Adrian designer. A one-off piece. She held the dress up in front of her in the mirror and smiled at how the colour added roses to her cheeks and brought out the chestnut tones in her hair.

She turned her head at a knock at the door and raised an eyebrow at Gio in question when he walked in.

'It's beautiful,' he said. 'Is that the one you've chosen?'

'I think so. What do you think it says about me?'

He smiled. 'That you look great in red?'

She rolled her eyes. 'I know you're more

savvy about the press than that. Does it send the right message?'

'This sends the message that you are beautiful and smart and accomplished.'

Which were all the right things to say, of course. Which made it more than a little suspicious.

'That's a talkative dress,' she observed, her voice sardonic.

'To be fair, it's your face that's saying most of it.'

'You're an exceptionally smooth talker, you know that?'

'How else would I have got you to agree to marry me?'

Hailey laughed, hanging the dress back on the rail. 'Do you really want me to answer that?'

He shook his head, smiling. 'No. I want you to come here and look at this. It's a good thing. I think. I hope.' He sat on the love seat in front of the window and patted the cushion beside him. 'Come, sit. Please?'

He pulled a small leather box from his pocket and for a moment she forgot to breathe. This was the part in the fairy tale where she was meant to swoon. And it might be clichéd, but she couldn't help but be slightly overwhelmed at the thought of him dropping to one knee while holding that tiny box.

'We talked about a ring,' he said, 'and if there's something in particular that you want then you only have to say. But I saw this in the family collection and it seemed so perfect for you…'

He looked up at her, and she recognised hope in his eyes. She took the box from his outstretched hand. The leather was warm from his skin and she turned it over a couple of times, not sure how she felt about it.

'You didn't have to do this,' she said. They'd talked about a ring, once, briefly. But, in the grand scheme of things, it just hadn't seemed important.

'We're about to announce our engagement. Trust me when I say you need a ring,' he said.

'But a family piece…'

'Is entirely appropriate for a woman who's about to become my family.'

She shook her head because there was just no chance that he could understand what she was feeling.

'What about my background?' she asked. Because he might think that it didn't matter, but he was wrong.

'What about it?' he asked, proving her point.

'The press are going to have a field day,' she said. 'Digging around. All those foster parents to pay for their stories. All those kids I shared children's homes with. My birth parents, wherever they are. My adoptive parents. I know I should have told them already. But it's too late for a Christmas card and I haven't picked up the phone and called them in over a year. I just can't do it.'

He reached for her fidgeting hands. Closed his around them, trapping the ring box inside.

'Does a family ring change that? Because we can absolutely choose something new. No weird family connections involved. But…'

'But?' she asked, not sure how he could possibly make wearing a piece of jewellery from the royal collection feel right on someone like her.

'But all of those things you're worried about would still be the case, regardless of which ring you choose. We've spoken to the press office about your past. They're handling it. Would you like to talk about it again?'

'No, no. That's not what I mean. It's just… I'm not the sort of person who's meant to wear a piece from the royal collection, am I?'

'You're the woman I'm marrying,' Gio said, pulling her closer, 'which is precisely why you are the right woman to wear a family ring.'

'This is precisely the problem, Gio. You're marrying me, but I'm not the sort of woman you *should* be marrying. And you know that your family agrees with me.'

'You're the woman I *want* to marry,' Gio argued. 'I feel like that should count for more than what my parents think. Isn't what *we* want more important?' he demanded.

It was so easy for him to say that. He wasn't the one who was going to be curtseying to the wrong duchesses and turning up to the polo match in the wrong shoes. If he thought that didn't matter, then he was being either hopelessly obtuse or naïve.

'I think that it will matter to the journalists who are going to slate me for every mistake. It matters to your friends and family, who will be laughing at me behind my back.'

Gio ran a hand through his hair again, a sure sign that he was reaching the end of his patience. 'Hailey, did you forget how we met? You know my friends. And you know that Sebastian thinks you're great.'

'Sebastian isn't your mother,' she pointed out.

'Why is my mother's approval so important?' He *was* being obtuse, because there was

no way that Gio could possibly be unaware
of the answer to that question.

'Because she's your mother, Gio, and the
Queen.'

'You're having doubts.' Gio said, which
was quite the leap from what she had said.
And a convenient way to turn this conversation back on itself.

'No, I'm not.' She couldn't have doubts
because she wasn't marrying Gio for herself, which meant that her feelings about his
mother didn't come into it. She was doing
this for their baby. 'I'm just starting to realise
what I've let myself in for. I thought I was
done with feeling like this,' she added with a
sigh. Because she might have no thoughts of
backing out but that didn't mean that she was
blind to the challenges that lay ahead of them.

'Like what?' Gio asked.

'Like the one who's always going to be
on the outside looking in. Always trying to
look like I belong when everyone knows that
I don't.'

'That's not how I feel,' Gio argued, taking her hand.

Hailey shook her head because that really
wasn't the point. 'It's not about feelings, Gio.
It's about facts. And one fact that we can be
certain of is that I'm never going to fit in with

your family. It doesn't change my mind. I still want to marry you. I suppose I'm just realising what that's going to mean for me.'

'My family isn't *our* family,' Gio said with an edge to his voice. '*Our* family is the three of us, and if being in Adria makes you feel that way then maybe we should think again about living somewhere else. Or maybe you really should reconsider whether marrying me is the right thing to do.'

'If I do that, our baby is going to grow up as an outsider too, and I can't do that to them. No. I know what I have to do, and I'm sorry for the wobble.'

'What you *have* to do? Hailey, you don't have to do anything that you don't want to. I don't want to marry someone who's only doing it because she feels she has no choice. Call me old-fashioned but I'd rather have someone who *wants* to marry me, even if it's not for romantic reasons.'

Hailey stared at him. 'But you're doing this for the same reason, let's not pretend that—'

Before she could finish her sentence, Gio had pulled her to him and slid his fingers into her hair. He tilted her face up to his and she resisted the urge to turn her cheek into the heat of his palm. Instead, she tipped her chin up, just a fraction, so that she could look him in the eye.

She took a breath, determined to finish her sentence, but before she could speak Gio's eyelashes swept closed, his chin dipped and his lips pressed hard against hers. She shivered as his fingertips curled into the short hairs at her nape, and wound her arms around his neck, pulling herself higher as Gio deepened the kiss, licking into her mouth, wrapping an arm tight around her waist and pinning her to his body, any thought of keeping her feet on the ground—either literally or metaphorically—long forgotten.

When he pulled away, taking in a great, heaving gasp of air, she realised that she was as far gone as he was, could feel the hot pink flush of her skin, the rapid beating of her heart and the gasp of rapid breaths.

She raised her eyebrows at Gio, not trusting herself to speak just yet.

'I'm marrying you because I want to,' he said by way of explanation. She had yet to find the capacity for speech, so had no choice but to let him go on. 'The fact that you're pregnant is part of that, of course it is. But you seem to have this idea that I'm acting out of some disinterested sense of duty. And, as

I think I have just made painfully clear, that couldn't be further from the truth.'

She stared up at him as he slowly loosened his arms but kept her close. 'But I thought… I didn't think that we were…' She floundered, unable to form a sentence. Because this was everything that she had told herself not to want. If they were going to add their *feelings* into this situation then she had no idea where it was heading. If she could tell herself that they were both doing this for the baby, then she could let herself believe that it was a good idea. That there was some version of the future that ended with a happy family life, rather than with her heart broken, piecing together the parts of her life that remained when Gio burned it to the ground.

But if this was going to get personal, if Gio was saying that he wanted *her*—just her, not her baby, not her as a mother to his child, or even a princess to his prince—if he wanted her then it was personal. It would be her, personally, who would be left broken when it all went wrong.

'We don't have to,' Gio said, his voice low and rough, almost breaking with barely contained emotion. 'If I misread things and this isn't what you want… If you want to pretend that this never happened and you're happier with the idea that I've not thought about you that way since that night, then fine. I can give you that. But I couldn't just let you make assumptions without…correcting them.'

'Consider me corrected,' she breathed, still not able to commit to a decision one way or another. On the one hand was Gio, and kissing, and the fact that she might expire from frustration if she didn't get him into the nearest bed very soon. And on the other…her heart. Which had been bruised so many times before that she couldn't bear the thought of exposing it again.

'So,' Gio asked gently. 'Is that what you want? To pretend this never happened? To go back to assuming that I'm doing this out of duty and nothing more? That I'm not thinking about leaning down and kissing you again right now?'

She shook her head because she couldn't deny what her body so clearly wanted. She didn't have it in her to lie at this moment. 'No. I don't want that,' she said. 'But that sounds a lot simpler than whatever it is you're suggesting.'

He nudged his nose against hers and she drew in a sharp breath at that intimacy. 'I'm suggesting we give this a try,' he murmured.

'Marriage,' she clarified. 'A real marriage. Not just…'

'Yes. Given that we're about to announce our engagement, and you're expecting my baby, resisting this attraction brings to mind sayings about horses bolting and stable doors.'

Attraction. Right. Of course. Hailey gave herself a mental slap to the side of the head. Not love; that would be ridiculous. Or affection, which would have been nice, she supposed. But at least attraction was simple. Straightforward. Gio was making it clear from the outset that this was about sex, and that was fine. That was as simple as duty, really, if she squinted at her own thoughts. This wasn't a love match and it never would be. She didn't have to worry about whether Gio was going to fall for her, because it had never been on the cards. But attraction—*that* she could return, safely, without risking anything getting broken. In that they were equal.

Her hands had come to rest against Gio's chest and she let them drift down to his hips, following the jut of his waist around to his back. She arched back against the arm at her waist, looking up at him thoughtfully.

'Resisting has been rather…energy-intensive,' Hailey conceded, as if the way she had bowed her body towards him at the first brush of his lips hadn't been perfectly eloquent without her saying a word. 'And as the pregnancy goes on, I can't imagine I'm going to have all that much energy to spare. So it would make sense, really…'

Gio raised an eyebrow at her. 'From a purely practical standpoint?'

'Right. Yes. From a purely practical standpoint I think that more—' she looked them both up and down, gestured between their bodies '—more of this would be acceptable.'

Gio huffed out a little laugh, hands coming to her cheeks, tipping her face up until she was looking him in the eye again.

'Acceptable,' he repeated, his voice breaking into a gravelly lilt that did something dangerous between her thighs. 'Are you quite sure that was the word you wanted to choose? Not, perhaps, irresistible, or something similar?'

Her lips quirked up in a smile that she tried to tamp down. There was no need to feed his ego any more than necessary. 'I think "acceptable" just about covers it,' she said, though it would have been more effective if her voice hadn't dropped to a breathy whisper.

'Then I see I need to try harder to impress you.'

Gio gave her one of his full-on smiles, and just like the first time she was lost in those

wrinkles around his eyes, the lines bracket-
ing his wide mouth and his even white teeth.

'Try as hard as you like,' she invited, tipping herself up towards him and letting out
a groan as his lips came down to meet hers.

CHAPTER NINE

ATTRACTION. THAT WAS safe enough, Gio told himself. He'd been dreaming—literally and metaphorically—about having Hailey back in his arms ever since that first night in New York. It couldn't be any more dangerous to claim her, surely.

He just had to remember that they were only talking about attraction here. No one had said anything about emotions being involved, and he knew better than to think someone might love him just because he loved them. So he would stop fighting this need he had to put his hands on Hailey, to have her lips on the stubble beneath his jaw or her breath in his ear as he kissed his way along her neck.

He just had to remember not to fall for her, because she couldn't have made it any clearer that she wouldn't be here at all if she hadn't been pregnant. She hadn't chosen him, or this life. She was making the best of it in order to give their baby the family she thought it deserved. He couldn't expect her to love him when not even his own family had managed that. Realistic expectations were the only thing that were going to keep his heart safe.

Hailey eased herself away from him just a fraction and they both glanced down at the dress that she was somehow still holding, which had been crushed between their bodies.

He loosened his arm around her waist and she took half a step back, away from him.

'I'm going to have to get this pressed,' she said with a look that caused a very self-satisfied grin to light up his face.

'I'm sorry if I inconvenienced you,' he said, and Hailey hit him gently in the chest, rolling her eyes.

'Don't fish for compliments. It's not dignified.'

He laughed, taking the dress from her, shaking out the worst of the creases and hanging it back on the rail.

'How are you feeling about the photographs? Is there anything else you need?'

'Can you get me a lifetime of experience in the public eye so that I don't feel quite so terrified?'

He smiled a little wistfully. 'I wouldn't wish that on you, darling.'

Darling? He didn't know where the endearment had come from. And it shouldn't have felt so natural on his lips. He refused to overthink it. It was just a word. Generic and impersonal, the sort of word anyone might use with a woman they had just thoroughly kissed. There was absolutely no reason for the hook he felt in his stomach.

'Then I suppose I'm as prepared as I am ever likely to be,' Hailey said, with no mention of his verbal slip. Perhaps she hadn't even noticed it. Perhaps she just assumed it meant nothing.

'You approve of the dress?' she asked.

'You don't need my approval.'

Hailey made a little huff of frustration. 'I'm asking you as an expert on press relations. Not as my fiancé.'

'Well, then,' Gio replied. 'In my role as your unofficial press advisor, I would say that the dress is an excellent choice. As your fiancé I would say that you look glowing and beautiful, but we both know that my opinion isn't important.'

She reached up and kissed him on the lips. A touch gentler, more comfortable, safer, than the one they had shared before.

'Thank you. Then I've got everything I need.'

They both looked around at the sound of a knock at the door.

'Hair and make-up are ready for Ms Thomas,' the chamberlain said when Gio called for him to enter.

'We just need a few minutes,' Gio said, glancing over his shoulder. 'We'll call you when Ms Thomas is ready.' He had almost forgotten that he had come in here with a task to accomplish, and he couldn't leave until it was done.

'Was there something else?' Hailey asked, her expression quizzical as the chamberlain snicked the door closed behind him. Gio picked up the ring box from the coffee table, where it had sat, forgotten, while they'd thrashed out how they felt about one another.

Dropping to one knee, he opened the box, held it up to Hailey and said, 'This is how I should have done this in the first place. Hailey Thomas, would you do me the great honour of agreeing to marry me?'

Hailey took the ring from the box, turning it over in her fingers as she followed the winding fern engraving around the delicate gold circlet.

'Gio, it's beautiful. Perfect. I love it.'

He smiled again, broadly, with a deep glow

of satisfaction that he knew her well enough to anticipate her reaction.

'When I saw it, I thought it could have been made for you. I hope I wasn't presumptuous.'

'Not at all,' she said, watching his face as he slid the ring onto her finger. 'I'm touched that you chose something so perfect. Yes, of course I will marry you.' He stood and glanced down as she let her hand rest on his chest, and the sight of the ring on her finger, a visible sign of the commitment they were making together, made something feel tight behind where her hand rested.

'I really do have to get ready,' Hailey said, looking him in the eye and letting her tongue flicker over her lips in a way that was absolutely not going to help that happen any time soon. He groaned, pressed a quick kiss to her lips and stepped away.

'I'll leave you to it,' he said. 'Have someone call me if you need anything.'

Hailey turned her hand in the light from the window. She had meant what she'd said to Gio just now—the ring was perfect. If he hadn't told her that it was a family piece, she could have believed that he had had it made for her.

Suddenly, with Gio's ring on her finger,

this whole thing felt real in a way that even having his child growing inside her hadn't yet achieved. When she walked out of the palace wearing his ring, that would be all anyone would be interested in. She was setting herself up for a life that was Gio-adjacent, and everything she did from that moment on would be judged on how well she integrated herself into his family. Well, she considered, at least she had already fulfilled her first obligation as a princess by getting pregnant. There was one thing, at least, that she couldn't be accused of failing at. Though no doubt once everyone realised that the date of conception roundly coincided with the date that she had met Gio, the tabloid press—and Gio's family—would have plenty to say about how a royal baby *should* be conceived.

Which, she was sure, would be right about when Gio changed his mind and started wondering how he could get himself out of the situation they were in. It had happened again and again through her childhood, sometimes after the first sleep-deprived night, when the nightmares that had followed her through a succession of homes had caused her to cry out in her sleep, waking other children, babies, pets. Foster parents who thought that taking in an older child would mean avoiding the night-time waking of an infant. Only to find by morning that an emotional, traumatised child was not the easy option.

Sometimes it had come after a month, or three. For a million reasons she'd forced herself not to care about because they all amounted to the same thing: none of them had wanted to keep her.

She had every reason to assume that her relationship with Gio would follow the exact same pattern. If she hadn't got pregnant their first night together, she would never have seen him again—she would be long forgotten by now.

She had tried to warn him off rushing into this marriage. But if he was going to insist on giving their baby everything that she wanted for it by marrying her and making them a family then she was going to take him up on it.

But she wasn't stupid enough to think that it would be for ever. Sure, there might never have been a divorce in the Adrian royal family, something that Gio had explained was the reason his parents were still married—and still miserable—but there were plenty of ways for Gio to send her back to New York without legally ending their marriage. He could stop coming home. He could simply just stop caring.

Whatever happened between them, wherever that kiss just now was heading, the most important thing she had to do now was remember that.

She could enjoy this now—she *should* enjoy this now. How often did you actually get to marry Prince Charming? But she could never lose sight of the fact that his feelings for her were only temporary.

She could give up a lot—her home, her business, her privacy—but she wasn't stupid enough to give up her heart. Protecting that was her last line of defence.

The photographs were being taken in the morning room, where they would be getting married in just a week. It was heavily decorated for the Christmas season, with boughs of greenery around the mirror behind the writing bureau, swagged pine wreaths across the fireplace and branching candelabras on side tables. An enormous tree had been erected in the corner beside the French windows and the natural light caught in the silver and crystal decorations.

A brocade-upholstered chaise had been pulled in front of the window, the low winter sun picking out the silver in the ivory fabric. Hailey hesitated after a footman showed her into the room, watching Gio where he was talking with the chamberlain and the photographer. He had had his own encounter with the hair and make-up team, it seemed. His curls were tucked neatly back after she had mussed them earlier, his stubble trimmed as short as she had seen it.

His suit was a sober charcoal three-piece, with a silver silk tie and snowy-white shirt that had been pressed to within an inch of its life. In short, there was nothing about him that would possibly betray the fact that there was a human under all that tailoring rather than something chiselled from cold, hard marble.

That was until he looked up and saw her, and one of those devastating grins spread across his features and her mind was cast dangerously back in time, to the night that they'd first met, when that smile had been her undoing.

And then she remembered. This was show-time. The photographer was here to capture the happy couple with their whirlwind romance— a much better cover for a shotgun wedding than a drunkenly and accidentally conceived illegitimate prince or princess. That was the reason for Gio's smile—he was playing the part of an adoring fiancé, she reminded herself, and he was waiting for her to do the same.

She crossed the room to him and accepted his kiss on both cheeks, before his fingertips found her chin and tipped her face up to his until she met his gaze. She felt her cheeks flush with heat at the look in his eyes.

'What's wrong?' Gio asked, clearly picking up on her discomfort, his hand on her cheek now.

'Nothing,' she said, wiping her face clear of whatever it was giving away. 'Just nervous, I suppose.'

'Don't be,' Gio said, his voice low. 'Just be yourself. That's all we need to show everyone.'

Not true, her brain protested. They needed to show the people what they wanted to see. Not the messy, real-life problems beneath it all.

Being herself had never been enough in the past, and it certainly wasn't going to be enough to navigate through this new royal life. What she needed to do was fake it. Because perhaps if she did that for long enough, this life would start to feel real and she could kid herself that she belonged in it. Maybe one day she might start to believe it.

She pasted a smile onto her face that she hoped looked more genuine than it felt, and met Gio's eyes before very deliberately stretching up onto her toes to kiss him on the lips.

'I'm fine.' She turned her smile onto the photographer. 'Should I sit?'

The photographer, his assistant and the hair and make-up team bundled her to the chaise and spent an inordinate amount of time tweaking pleats and placing hands and checking light levels. She was aware that she was sitting as if she had a stick up her arse, and that in this position her dress probably wasn't doing a great job of hiding their little secret.

Every time the camera clicked she flinched, and her grip on Gio where their fingers were entwined went a little more white-knuckled.

Until Gio lifted their linked hands to his lips while the photographer checked something on his laptop.

'You either need to tell me what's wrong or find me a paramedic, darling,' Gio said quietly in her ear. 'Because if you squeeze any tighter, bones are going to start breaking.' She tried to snatch her hand away, but Gio captured it in his, pressing a kiss to the centre of her palm.

As she tried to process his words, from the corner of her eye she caught sight of a bare patch in one of the garlands. The mistletoe had lost its berries, and leaves had been crushed where someone had been heavy-handed when it was installed.

'What's wrong?' Gio asked, following the line of her gaze to the fireplace.

'Nothing's wrong,' she said on reflex.

Gio arched an eyebrow. 'Are you sure about that? You seem to be staring.'

She grunted quietly with frustration. 'Okay, fine. There's a bare patch in the garland over there. It's annoying me and I can't concentrate. But it's fine. Probably no one else would even notice.'

'But you've noticed, and it's bothering you,' he said, his voice maddeningly reasonable.

She shrugged. 'It's fine, okay? Just drop it.'

'Look, if you want to fix the garland, you should fix the garland,' Gio said.

'We're in the middle of a photoshoot,' she hissed from the corner of her mouth, trying not to move from the position the photographer had finally deemed acceptable. 'I just want to get this over with.'

'They'll wait,' Gio said, his voice terse. 'You just said yourself you're not happy with how it's going. The great thing about marrying me—'

She snorted half a laugh—she couldn't help it.

'The great thing about marrying me,' Gio went on, though with a twinkle in his eye, 'is that you sometimes get things to be just how you want them. Take advantage of that. If you want to fix the garland, we'll put things on hold while you get it how you want it.'

She glanced at the photographer and then rolled her eyes. 'Fine, well, if I am marrying you, there should at least be some perks.' But she couldn't deny that the corners of her lips were turning up.

'We're taking a break,' Gio said, standing from the chaise and holding his hand out for Hailey. She slipped her hand into his and followed him across the room to the fireplace.

With the grand dimensions of the room, the garland was at head height and she had to strain her neck to properly see the strands that were bothering her.

'Need a hand?' Gio asked.

'Something to stand on,' she said, looking around.

'Aha,' Gio said, before returning with an upholstered footstool.

She raised a brow at him. 'I'm not standing on an antique.'

'It's fine. It's ugly and I don't want to inherit it anyway,' he said, making her laugh.

She wavered, but then kicked off her shoes. She tested the surface with her toes before tentatively stepping up, before Gio's hands came to rest on her waist.

'What are you doing?' she asked, spinning on the spot and nearly toppling off the stool in the process.

'Making sure you don't fall,' Gio said, his face straight. 'And a good job too, by the looks of it.'

'That was only because you—' she started, before Gio interrupted.

'I'm not risking you falling—not risking you or the baby. I'm planning on being horribly over-protective of you both; you'd better get used to the idea.'

She snorted at his overreaction but didn't move away. And it took probably more moments than it should for her to realise that she was still standing with her body pressed against his, with no real inclination to move. Not when the heat had returned to Gio's eyes and she felt herself warming under his appraisal.

'I should...' she started, but she couldn't really find the motivation to finish the sentence, not when she was doing what she had been thinking of doing since that kiss earlier, and with the audience still on the other side of the room there was no reason not to indulge the impulse to be close to him. They were meant to be madly in love—pressing herself against him and not denying how irresistible he was to her was practically her job now. As long as she didn't start to believe it herself, she was fine. She could play with it, and why not play with something that felt so good?

For the first time she was eye to eye with him, and suddenly the stool didn't seem so bad after all. She decided she quite liked it as she let herself drift towards him, let her lips brush against his. He smiled against her mouth and she took in his expression as she pulled her body away from his.

'I need to fix this garland,' she said, her voice soft.

'Uh-huh,' Gio managed, looking a little dazed. She turned and his hands stayed on her hips as she rethreaded the strands of the greenery that made up the bough, borrowing a sprig of berries from further along the garland and twisting leaves and stalks to hide the areas that had been crushed. She leant away from the fireplace and into Gio's shoulder to take in the effect.

'Better?' she asked.

'Much,' Gio answered, his lips close to her ear as his arms wrapped around her waist.

She snorted a laugh at him, but relaxed against his body as she took in her handiwork.

'You're meant to be looking at the garland,' she reminded him.

'Of course.' But his arms tightened around her waist and his lips pressed to her neck, and she suspected that he had about as much interest in the greenery as she did right now—which was close to zero.

A subtle clearing of throats from behind them snapped her out of whatever trance being so close to Gio's body had provoked. And if it hadn't been for his steadying hands on her hips she was quite sure that she would have lost her footing while performing an inelegant leap down from the stool. Somehow, despite the fact that having an audience had given her permission to let her feelings for Gio show for once, she'd quite forgotten that they were there once his body was close enough to hers that she could feel the heat of it even through the layers of starched cotton and brushed fine wool he was wearing.

'I'm sorry,' she said, walking back towards the chaise. 'Should I sit back where—?'

'Actually, Your Royal Highness,' the photographer said, addressing Gio, 'if you'll forgive me, I took the liberty while you were adjusting the floral arrangement, and I thought you might like to take a look...'

With more than a little trepidation, Hailey looked at the photographer's laptop as he drew up a couple of the shots. There was no denying that they were…compelling.

The red of her dress against the green of the pine boughs was undeniably festive, and the natural light combined with the candelabras either side of the fireplace was beautifully soft and atmospheric. But that was nothing compared to the warmth that was so obvious between her and Gio. As she'd leaned back against his shoulder and they'd shared a heated look. The way he'd watched her, hands anchoring her as she'd leaned to tweak the garland. The way that her body had been plastered against his from shoulder to knees, when she'd turned in his arms and he'd lowered her to the floor.

They looked very much…into one another. They were almost too revealing, Hailey thought, studying the expression on the face of the Hailey on the screen. The one who was staring into Gio's eyes as if no one else in the world existed.

But that was the story, she reminded herself. She and Gio might not have exactly worked out how this marriage of theirs was going to work, but what they had agreed on was that they wanted his family and the rest of the world to believe they were madly in love. And these photos…well, they certainly got the job done. And if it meant that she could get on with the rest of the day without having to sit stiffly on that chaise for a moment longer, then she was going to jump at the opportunity.

'These look wonderful,' she said, glancing up at Gio to make sure that they were on the same page. 'I'm happy if you are,' she added, waiting—and waiting—for him to respond. His gaze was fixed firmly on the screen, and in the end she resorted to slipping an arm around his waist in a less than subtle attempt to get his attention.

'Yes. Perfectly fine,' he said at last. 'I think we can wrap things up here.' And with that he strode from the room, leaving her bewildered in a room full of strangers.

'If you'll excuse me,' Hailey said to the photographer, hoping that she didn't sound quite as abandoned as she felt.

She walked from the room, wondering whether she should try and find Gio—what she would say to him when she did. Was he afraid, as she was, that those pictures had revealed too much? That in an unguarded moment they had revealed that this marriage was more real than either of them had intended? And if that was the case—if the feelings were real—where did that leave them?

Because this had seemed so much simpler when they were both telling themselves—and each other—that they were only doing this for the baby's sake.

Before she had seen that look in Gio's eyes in the photos, so similar to the expression in her own. It made it so much harder to remember that this was all temporary—the attraction and, she didn't know, affection—that was between them, even if the legal marriage part meant that she was signing up to be around for the long haul. But the only way she could make that work was by making sure that she remembered that whatever Gio thought he might be feeling for her now, it wouldn't—couldn't—last. But if those pictures had been of anyone else—if they had been strangers, rather than herself and the man she was about to marry, she would have said that the feelings she could see between them looked very much like love.

But that was absurd. She couldn't love Gio. She'd only known him a few months, had spent barely a month of that time in his company. She lusted after him, sure. Fantasised about him. Thought about the night they had spent together and dreamed about it happening again. But she couldn't love him. *Couldn't*. Because this marriage was supposed to be simple—a way of giving her child the family life she wanted it to have. It was not meant to have anything to do with how she might feel about Gio personally.

The best thing that she could do about those feelings was bury them as deep as she could and pretend they'd never existed. And as for the rest of it—the kiss they'd shared earlier that day, how she'd felt with Gio's body hard against hers... Well, she'd not had feelings for Gio the one night they'd gone to bed together, any more than he'd had feelings for her. So there was no reason to conflate the two. They could kiss, or more, if they both wanted, without it meaning any more than it had that first night. And, hell, maybe it would make things easier if they weren't trying to deny what they wanted on that front. They were going to be married. She wanted that marriage to last. And she knew that she could do that without Gio loving her—she had never expected that in the first place—but she wasn't sure that she could be married to him without wanting him. And it seemed as if they were reaching their limits on how long they could ignore that want.

She retraced her steps through the palace and found the door to their bedroom ajar, Gio sitting on the edge of the bed with his jacket discarded, tie loosened and hair curling rebelliously around his ears again.

'Hey,' she said from the doorway, and Gio looked up, clearly startled.

'Hailey,' he said, his voice cracking.

'Everything okay?' she asked. 'You left so quickly...' She crossed to the bed, planning on sitting beside him, but Gio caught her by the hips and pulled her between his legs, bringing them eye-to-eye again.

'I think we need to talk about how this marriage is going to work,' he said gruffly.

'Funny,' Hailey said, cupping his jaw and moving closer. 'I was thinking the same.'

'I want you,' Gio said bluntly, as if she didn't know it already. 'And when I saw those photos, I don't know... Maybe I'm just seeing what I want to see, but I think you feel the same. And that makes it so much harder to hold back from what I really want to do.'

'And what is it you want to do?' she asked, letting her hand stray round to his hair, where it was coming undone, threading her fingers into his curls and turning his face to her.

'This all started with me wanting you,' he said. 'With not being able to follow what was going on in that meeting because I couldn't stop looking at you.'

'Oh, and here was me thinking that this

started with you yawning through my very important client presentation.' Hailey tried to make light of it, but her voice shook, and she knew there was no way of avoiding the conversation they were about to have.

Gio pulled her even closer, wrapping his arms around her waist and letting his forehead rest against her collarbone. 'Please, don't remind me. I thought you'd forgiven me for that.'

'Oh, I don't know,' she said, turning and pressing a kiss to the side of his head. 'If this is the reaction I get, I might bring it up more often.'

He pressed a kiss against her collarbone and she gasped. She felt his lips curl into a smile against her shoulder and didn't have to look down to know how his expression would have changed into something dangerous.

'We're getting married next week,' he said, brushing a kiss against the side of her neck that drew another gasp from her as she dug her fingers deeper into his hair.

'We are,' she agreed, tipping her head to one side to grant greater access where his lips were tracing up the side of her neck. His grip around her waist had loosened, and one hand ran down the smooth satin of her skirt, fingering the pleats until his fingertips found the hem at her calves and slid the fabric up, up, until he reached the bare skin at the top of her thigh and he groaned.

'Gio,' she said, her voice sounding distant, even to her own ears.

'Hmm,' he replied, and she felt it as a hum against her skin.

'I think maybe we were talking.'

'Mmm…' he said, and she felt the vibration of his lips all the way down to her thighs.

'And I think we should maybe finish that conversation before this goes any further.'

He paused, and her skin felt chilled where his lips had touched. He glanced up and met her eyes. 'Is that conversation going to conclude that we both want this to go where it is clearly going?'

'Well, yes, but—'

'Then isn't *afterwards* as good a time as any to have that conversation?'

Did he know that the soft touch of his fingertips around the top of her stocking was making it completely impossible to think? She had to suspect that he did, and yet she found no interest in stopping him. He was right. If this was inevitable, it didn't really matter whether they talked before or after.

Several hours later, as she tucked her chin onto his chest and struggled to stop herself falling asleep, she wondered why they had waited so long to do this again. Surely nothing that felt so good could be a mistake. And yet…

That was the problem, wasn't it? Because some parts of their life *did* feel so good, and yet others…too good to be true. Bathed in sweat and hormones and afterglow, and without the conversation she was sure that they needed to have, it would be too easy to forget all the things she'd been reminding herself of since she had got here. That she couldn't let herself fall for Gio. No matter how good or how right it felt lying here, with his shoulder for a pillow and his child growing inside her. Sooner or later, his affections would falter and the only way to survive that would be to protect herself from feeling too much. Now was the time she had to fortify those walls, make sure that she was strong enough to be with him, to give their baby the family it deserved, without letting herself get too hurt when it all ended.

CHAPTER TEN

HAILEY WOKE TO a light knock at the door, and a morning greeting from a maid, and as she was pushing herself up on her pillows and rubbing the sleep from her eyes she remembered that it was Christmas Day. She crossed to open the curtains. And a moment after that she remembered that she and Gio shared a bed now, and realised that on their first Christmas morning together they weren't waking up together.

They'd eaten supper in their apartment the night before, once they'd dragged themselves out of bed, eschewing the big family feast, knowing that they would be spending hours around the table today. And Gio had even skipped out on midnight mass, which she was sure they would pay for when they saw his parents today. But it had been inevitable really, that one time together wasn't going to be enough, and that it would be worth paying the price of skipping out on royal engagements as long as they were there for the *cenone* tomorrow—the big meal that the day revolved around. Today. Just a whole afternoon and evening with her soon-to-be in-laws, who she was pretty certain hated her already, and who she knew treated Gio so poorly. But this was the price she paid for giving their baby a family with a mother and a father and a safe home and a place in the world.

The whole point of being here was to be *with* Gio. So why wasn't he here? It wasn't exactly something she could ask the staff, and the very fact that she even had staff was something she could never get used to.

She showered and dressed slowly, not sure whether she was missing some important family breakfast or something, but there was no way she was leaving this room without Gio by her side to protect her.

Just as she was about ready to renounce their engagement and run off back to New York, Gio turned up with a tray full of toast and tea, and if she wasn't already planning on marrying him in less than a week, that could have been the deciding vote.

'Thought you might want something to eat before you have to face my family, so I raided the kitchens,' he said, placing the tray on her dressing table and catching her by the hand. He reeled her in, slid a hand to the short hair at the nape of her neck and pulled gently. She looked up and melted. It was unfortunate to have a fiancé so irresistible, even when you were mad at him.

'I was cross with you,' she murmured against his lips.

'I'm sorry. I didn't think you'd wake before I got back,' he said. 'You were sleeping so deeply when I left.'

'Well, I was tired, for some reason.' She gave him a smirk and was rewarded with a boyish grin.

'Will I be forgiven if I give you your Christmas present? We usually exchange gifts after lunch, but I'd rather it was just us here.'

'A gift?' Hailey asked, surprised. Between the baby and the wedding and moving halfway across the world in the space of a couple of weeks, Christmas presents had been so far down her agenda that they had fallen off the bottom completely. 'You can't, Gio,' she exclaimed. 'I haven't got you anything. I didn't even think.'

'Would it make you feel better if I told you that it was more of a…a loan than a gift?'

She frowned, both confused and intrigued. 'What do you mean?'

He grabbed her hand and pulled her into their sitting room, where a cloth was draped over something that could only be a picture frame, standing on a very dignified-looking gold easel.

'Gio…what have you done?' she asked nervously.

'It's just a loan,' he reminded her, pulling her by the hand until they were standing in front of the easel.

She reached out slowly for the gold draped cloth and pulled. In the second before it fell she knew what painting it was going to be, and her heart dropped into her stomach.

'Gio, you didn't— You can't— What did you do?' Because this painting was supposed to be in New York, at the exhibition she'd wished she'd been able to attend before she'd left. The one that she'd mentioned in passing to Gio, and she'd had no idea that he'd remembered.

'I didn't buy it,' Gio said ruefully. 'The museum wouldn't sell,' he told her, and at the thought that he'd even tried to buy it for her, something in her brain exploded. 'But we have it on loan, for our apartment. For a year. I had to promise that it could feature in a few exhibitions, but for most of the time it's yours to look at whenever you want.'

She glanced between the painting and Gio; neither seemed quite real in that moment. She reached out a finger to feel the brush strokes in the oil paint, but pulled herself back at the last moment, remembering that this was a priceless four-hundred-year-old masterpiece.

'I don't think I'm ever going to be able to stop looking at it,' she said, as tears filled her eyes and Gio's arm found its way around her waist. She leaned into his side, letting his arm take the weight of her head as she gazed at the painting. 'How did you know?'

'The way that you looked at the poster in New York. The way you so carefully tried to hide how much it meant to you. It was just a suspicion, but I'm glad that I was right. Merry Christmas,' he added, dropping his head to kiss her.

She groaned into his mouth and deepened their kiss, her arms coming around his waist as he lifted her closer. 'You like it?' Gio asked, and there it was; the doubt in his voice was what it took to tear her gaze away from the most beautiful thing she had ever seen.

'Gio,' she said seriously. 'I love it. It's the most astonishing thing I've ever seen. It's the most astonishing thing anyone has ever done for me. I *love* it,' she said again, her words heavy with emotion.

'So, is there any fallout from yesterday?' she asked when they eventually broke apart. 'Are your parents angry that we didn't come to dinner? Or church?'

He nodded. 'Yes. But I don't regret it. They'll have plenty of us today.'

She stifled a groan at the thought of it. 'I'm glad you don't regret it. I don't either. But is this where we have the conversation we didn't finish yesterday?'

'If you want to.' What she really wanted to do was spend the day gazing at her painting, but unfortunately they were living in the real world, with Gio's real family to face, and she didn't think she could do that until they knew where they stood with one another. 'I think we both need to know what this means to us, but there's no point having that conversation unless both of us want to.'

'Then yes. I want to. I'm sorry I didn't say that,' Hailey replied, and then took a deep breath. 'Was yesterday just a physical thing for you?'

'I don't see that it can be just physical,' Gio replied. 'Not when we're getting married in less than a week.'

'So it's more than that?' she asked.

Gio pulled them over to sit on the couch. 'You're asking a lot of questions and not offering much in return,' he observed, which was a fair observation, but he wasn't exactly being forthcoming about his feelings either.

'Yes. Well. Not knowing what to say is an unfortunate side effect of not knowing what I'm thinking,' Hailey told him. 'Or feeling. Everything seems so complicated.'

'So let's make it less complicated,' Gio suggested, as if that was something that they could realistically do. 'If I weren't me. If we didn't have to worry about my family trying to marry me off to the nearest available countess, then what would we be doing right now?' he asked.

'We already know the answer to that,' Hailey reminded him. 'We wouldn't have seen each other after that one night in New York.'

'We would, because of the baby. I wouldn't want to change that.'

'Then…' Hailey thought about it, tried to remove some of the complications of their situation to see what would be left if she and Gio were just… Hailey and Gio. 'I suppose we'd have got to know one another. Tried to be friends,' she said.

'And when those friends realised that they both still…*wanted* each other?'

She tried to remember how this worked in the real world. In her real life. In the before times. 'Then I guess…friends with benefits,' she said, her eyebrow raised.

'Not dating?' Gio clarified, in a cold, tense voice that made her wonder whether she'd just made a mistake.

'I never really did the dating thing,' she offered by way of explanation. But she could see the hurt in Gio's eyes, and didn't know how, or if, she could fix it.

'Is "friends with benefits" compatible with marriage?' Gio asked, still with that strained quality to his voice.

Hailey shook her head, not sure that this conversation was going how she'd intended, and equally unsure of how to get it back on track. 'A married couple who are friends is probably not the worst basis for a relationship,' she suggested, trying to look for the positives.

The *best* start to a marriage was probably 'madly in love, can't live without you', she supposed. But that didn't seem to be on the cards for her and Gio. So maybe they could make this marriage work like this. By being friends, and not fighting the fact that they wanted to fall into bed together at the end of the day. Or the middle of the day. Or—she glanced at the clock on the mantelpiece, wondering at what time they would be expected to make an appearance—at the start of the day, for that matter.

She placed her cup of tea carefully on the table beside the sofa and reached for Gio, pushed him back, settling herself comfortably across his thighs. 'I think I like being your friend,' she said with a tentative smile, hoping that The Talk hadn't spoilt things between them. She leaned down and kissed him. 'I love my gift. I'm sorry I didn't think to get you one.'

Gio arched an eyebrow, palms smoothing up her thighs. 'Merry Christmas to me,' he said, the start of a smile turning up the corners of his mouth. 'If you want to give me a last-minute gift, I'm sure we can think of something.'

His palm found the curve of her bottom, pulling her down more heavily on top of him.

'Shouldn't we...' she asked between kisses '...be going downstairs?'

'I think this would be awkward with an audience,' Gio said, pulling her close by the nape of her neck and kissing her until Hailey sat up abruptly, pulled her dress over her head, and found his mouth again with hers.

By the time they made it downstairs, Gio's family were sitting around the Christmas tree in the drawing room, sipping coffee and making polite conversation.

She had no doubt that his family knew exactly why they had missed breakfast that morning. Why they had missed dinner last night, and midnight mass too. She searched for something to say to the people who would become her family in less than a week. How many times had she done this before? she wondered. Met a new family at breakfast and found that she had no idea what to say to them. No idea how to belong. No idea how to make them love her. To make them want to keep her.

It was only the warm, smooth slide of Gio's fingers tangling with hers that reminded her that there was one very important difference now—this time she wasn't alone.

Gio wanted her here. For now, at least, she belonged with Gio, even if she didn't feel at home in the palace yet. And Gio would help her.

She squeezed his hand in silent thanks as Gio wished his parents a Happy Christmas and engaged them in small talk as Hailey looked on, happy to be on the edges of the conversation. To observe Gio and appreciate the way he tried to make her comfortable here in her new home, with her new family.

She refused the cup of coffee she was offered, mentally calculating how many cups she'd consumed in the last twenty-four hours, and had to suppress a smile as Gio pulled aside a member of staff and instructed them in how *exactly* she liked her tea prepared. She hadn't even realised he had been paying attention.

There was a warm glow in her chest at that knowledge—that didn't seem to fit with either 'convenient marriage' or 'friends with benefits'. Something that felt bigger and scarier than either of those and—accordingly—she planned to ignore it in perpetuity.

When they all moved to the big table in the dining room, with crystal, polished silverware and floral arrangements just a little higher than she would have designed, she realised with a sudden flash of horror that she and Gio hadn't been seated together. Of course, she remembered, it wouldn't do for the aristocracy to sit next to their own spouses at the dinner table.

But, with a squeeze of her hand, Gio pocketed the place card of the cousin who had been seated beside her.

'Gio,' she hissed under her breath. 'You can't.'

'I'm not leaving your side. Not with these sharks circling,' he whispered, pulling her into her seat, throwing his arm across the back of her chair and easing her closer to him with his fingertips on her shoulder.

'Tell me about the centrepieces,' he said, and her eyes snapped to his with surprise.

'Why do you want to know about the centrepieces?' she asked, suspicious—she could feel her own frown, the crease between her eyebrows.

'I don't care about the centrepieces,' Gio said. 'I want to see you talk.'

He wanted to watch her mouth. She remembered now that he'd done that the night they'd met. Well, how could she refuse an invitation to be worshipped doing something that she loved?

'Oh, you want to hear all about the *lisianthus* and the *zinnia*, do you?' she asked, over-enunciating and rolling her eyes as he set his elbow on the table, rested his chin on his hand and settled in to watch her talk.

She explained the different blooms and foliage, the meanings of each, which had to have been imported or grown in hothouses. She knew that Gio couldn't have developed a sudden interest in floristry, and yet his eyes were fixed on hers with unwavering focus. She flushed at the knowledge of how much he plainly desired her. The novelty of that hadn't worn off, and she didn't expect it to any time soon. She had barely got started with exploring Gio's body, with fully exploring all the things that he could do with hers.

Gio was her friend—he had every right to look at her that way after everything they had done over the last twenty-four hours, full of promise of what would come later. After denying how much she wanted him, she was suddenly intoxicated with the knowledge that she didn't have to any more. She could look. He could look. They could make all sorts of promises with their eyes, with every intention of collecting—and delivering—just as soon as they were alone together.

It was only when she realised that the room had gone quiet that she glanced around and realised that their conversation had not gone unnoticed. She felt heat rush to her cheeks again.

Sure, it worked in their favour for Gio's family to think that they were enamoured of each other. They were meant to be so in love that they couldn't wait to be married. But she had a more than sneaking suspicion that what was showing on her face wasn't exactly 'romantic'.

Well, it was too late to worry about that now, she told herself. His parents already knew she was pregnant. It wasn't as if she was planning on playing the blushing virgin on her wedding day.

CHAPTER ELEVEN

HE DIDN'T HAVE to pretend any more. The thrill of that had been coursing through his body since yesterday. A heady, potent force that held as much sway over him as the knowledge that he was going to be a father.

All he had to do now was keep their new 'friends with benefits' arrangement clear in his mind and ensure that he didn't start to kid himself that Hailey felt more than friendship towards him. Married or not. They weren't… romantic with one another. He had to remind himself that whatever this looked like from the outside—whatever they *had* to make it look like from the outside—Hailey didn't feel that way about him. Wasn't going to fall in love with him.

When they'd had their long-overdue conversation about what they were to each other in private, behind the public façade of their marriage, she hadn't even been able to go as far as dating. She'd gone straight to 'friends'. Sex, yes. Feelings, no. Which was absolutely acceptable, because it would never occur to him to hope for more. Even his own parents had been unable to form an emotional attachment to him. He supposed he should be grateful for the circumstances that meant Hailey would be bonded to him—committed to a life with him, even if only for the baby's sake. Because he knew he didn't have any chance of keeping her without it.

For the first time in his life he had a view of the future that was less lonely than the life he'd led until now.

But that didn't mean he could let his guard down. He'd learned over the years how to protect himself. Which barriers he needed to build and later reinforce if he didn't want his parents' indifference to his happiness to hurt him at every turn.

He had managed to thwart his parents' plan to have the choice of his spouse made by the royal council. And, against the expectations he'd had all his life, he'd chosen the woman he wanted to marry. But that didn't mean it was going to be smooth sailing from here.

The first, and most prominent, problem was the fact that he had no idea how to be a husband. A father. All his life he'd watched his parents fulfil their duties—to their country, to one another, to him—and in none of it had he ever seen an example that he wanted to follow. How to balance the obligations of state and family. How to maintain a cordial, affectionate relationship. How to treat the person your life was tied to when your relationship was based more on obligation than love.

He'd dreaded being forced to marry someone he didn't like, or barely knew. But he realised now, too late, that he'd never given enough thought to what came after. To what made a good marriage. All he knew was what he *didn't* want. So perhaps they got to start this with a clean slate. They could choose what would make their marriage happy. Right now, he couldn't think of anything that he wanted more than to watch her talk about flowers. The way her eyes lit and her words flew from her lips as she described what she would have done with the table. The work of art she would have created if this had been her commission. Until suddenly the joy faded from her eyes, and it didn't take thirty years of marriage to guess why.

'You're thinking about your business,' he guessed.

She nodded. 'I know I'm hardly the first person to have to give up her business because she got pregnant. I knew when I accepted your proposal what it would mean. But I just don't know what I'm meant to do with myself. At least until the baby comes.'

'I never said you have to give up your business,' Gio pointed out.

'No, but I don't see a solution for how I'm meant to run it from three thousand miles away. I keep going round and round in circles without finding a solution. I think maybe I should just give the business to Gracie. She's the only one I would trust to look after my clients.'

'You're aware that we have flowers in Adria.' He glanced at the arrangement in front of them. 'I never expected that you would give up work. If you want to, that's one thing. But you shouldn't have to make a sacrifice like that if it's not what you want.'

'I don't know what I'm going to want when the baby arrives. But I've spent a decade building that business. I can't just…forget about it. No matter the obligations I have here.'

Obligations. Well, that told him everything he needed to know about what this marriage was to her, and he felt a sinking sensation in the pit of his belly. He tried to avoid the—

'So, Gio, Hailey?' His mother's voice cut

through his thoughts and, for the first time in what felt like an hour, he tore his eyes away from Hailey and glanced down the dining table to the Queen.

'How are the wedding plans going?' she asked, and he suppressed the urge to roll his eyes.

He swore, from the minute they had announced their intention to marry, no one had shown the least bit of interest in any other part of their lives. It didn't matter how many times they'd asked them their preferences— how many times they'd told everyone around them that they didn't mind about the details as long as they were married at the end of the day, no one seemed to engage Hailey in conversation about anything other than the wedding.

'No change from yesterday,' he told his mother, trying to keep the annoyance out of his voice.

'I hear you are doing the flowers yourself. It's such a novelty to have someone with a trade join the family,' Queen Lucia said to Hailey, who looked startled at being addressed directly. She opened her mouth, closed it again, and Gio laid his hand over hers as he addressed his mother.

'That's enough,' Gio said, sending a sharp

look at his mother. 'Hailey is a world-renowned floral artist. She just did the flowers for Sebastian's wedding—it's how we met. No one could do a better job.'

He stood abruptly, his chair toppling behind him. 'I was very clear when Hailey and I arrived,' Gio continued, 'that my continued presence in this family is dependent on you both treating her with kindness and respect. I will not tolerate her being spoken to like that.' When he glanced across, it was to find Hailey standing beside him, wide-eyed with surprise. He reached for her hand. 'If you're finished, darling,' he said to her, 'I think it's time we retired.'

Her cheeks flushed and she nodded. 'Let's go.' He kept hold of her hand as they walked slowly from the room, not betraying the strength of his anger at the way his family had treated them. But as soon as they were out of sight of the dining room, he pulled them through a door hidden in the panelling of the corridor and crowded her up against the wall.

'I thought we were going back to our apartment,' she said, but let her head drop back against the wall as his hands came to land on her hips and he allowed his body to bow into hers until she was pinned by his weight.

The blaze in her eyes was hotter than ever, and she curled her fingers into the front of his jacket, leaving him in no doubt that her thoughts matched his entirely.

'I'm not sure I can wait,' Gio said, aware of the crack in his voice, not caring that it exposed exactly how much he wanted her.

'For what?' Hailey asked with mock innocence. The tight grip of her hands on his lapels pulling him down to her told a different story. She let her head fall to one side, exposing the long elegant line of her throat, and he couldn't resist dropping his lips there, letting them linger, brushing them against the sea of goosebumps that spread across her skin.

'Mmm…' she moaned, one hand leaving his sweater to thread in his hair, holding his lips to her skin, and gasping when his teeth and tongue followed the path of his lips.

'We should really be somewhere more private,' she said, and he nipped at her and smiled.

'That sounds promising. I want more than just the privacy of our apartment, though. Let's get away from here for a few days.'

She laughed, pushing him away. 'What are you talking about? We can't just disappear.'

'We can be in front of the fire at the ski lodge, completely alone, not another human in sight, in less than an hour if we take the helicopter. Say yes. Please?'

The corners of her mouth twitched up, and he knew that he had her. He wrapped his fingers around her wrist and pulled her behind him as he made his way through the dark corridors without a moment of hesitation.

Later that night, with Hailey's head cushioned comfortably on his shoulder, blankets, throws and furs pulled around them in the nest they'd made in front of the fire, Gio thought back to that expression on her face when his mother had been so cutting to her at the dinner table. How it had made him realise how little he knew her. How hard it would be to be a good husband to her if he didn't rectify that.

'I'm sorry about my mother,' he said, coiling one of her curls around his finger. Letting it slip from his grip as she looked up and propped her chin on his chest.

'It was nothing.'

He frowned. 'I don't think it was. It upsets me that she hurt you.'

'She didn't,' Hailey said, but from the tone of her voice it sounded as if the words came more from habit than honesty. He wanted her to be honest with him—needed it, if he were honest. If they wanted this marriage to turn out better than his parents' had.

'I want to know you better,' he told her, and felt the muscles of her back stiffen under his hand. 'I want to be a good husband,' he pressed on. 'I'm not sure that I know how to do that, if I'm perfectly honest. But I do want to try. I hate seeing pain in your eyes and not understanding it. Not knowing how I can help.'

Hailey was silent, and for a moment he worried that he'd pushed too far. Maybe with their whole 'friends with benefits' agreement he shouldn't be pressing for deep and mean-ingful conversations. But eventually Hailey settled down into his shoulder again and he held his breath, waiting for her to speak.

CHAPTER TWELVE

HAILEY HADN'T REALISED that Gio had seen her reaction when his mother had spoken to her as if she were some sort of interloper—the help who had somehow found herself invited to dinner. She'd done it with all of Gio's extended family looking on. And it had reminded her of every family meal she'd had to grit her teeth and get through before.

And Gio had seen, but not known what had caused it. He wanted to know, wanted to know her, and it struck her suddenly that she could just…tell him, share with him what she had felt. And have someone on her side. Someone who would go out of their way to make her welcome. Someone who she knew belonged on her side.

She closed her eyes and trusted herself, trusted Gio, and started to speak.

'It reminded me of being a child,' she said,

but then faltered. She still wasn't sure how to tell this.

'Can you tell me more?' Gio asked gently, his hand stroking slowly up and down her back, stopping occasionally to ease a knot in her muscle, or tuck the sheets and blankets a little more snugly around her shoulder.

'I lived in a lot of different places. With a lot of different families,' she told him. 'And… I never belonged. To start with, I would try so hard. Then I'd give up. Then I'd try twice as hard to be good.' And it would hurt twice as much when that still didn't work and she was still on the outside, trying to work out what it would take to actually belong in one of those families.

'It never worked. Even when I was eventually adopted I… It was too late. I'd never had a family of my own. I'd grown up without one, and I couldn't make myself fit. So when your mother looked at me like that, and spoke to me like that, it just brought back memories. That's all.'

She tucked herself into his shoulder a little tighter, although the fire was still burning hot beside them and their blanket nest was more than a match for the chill in the air. He wrapped his arms around her waist, press-

ing a kiss to the top of her head. He wanted
her to be in no doubt that she belonged here,
in his bed, in his arms, no matter what they
called it, either to themselves or to the outside world. They were a family, the three of
them, and they belonged together.

'I'm so sorry,' he said. 'That sounds hard,
and I'm sorry that my mother made you feel
like you don't belong here.'

If only it could be like this all the time,
just the two of them in an isolated lodge, un-
reachable except by helicopter, not a parent
or politician in sight.

'It's hardly news,' Hailey said, and he could
feel her forcing her face into a smile. He
looked down at her, at the warmth of her skin
in the reflected light of the fire, and cupped
her cheek with his hand until she looked up
and she met his eyes.

'You belong here,' he said, and the resolu-
tion in his voice hit her somewhere deep in
her chest. So she forced out a laugh because
that was easier than acknowledging how she
was really feeling.

'Right. The orphaned flower-seller from
the city, installed in the royal family. I remember that one.'

'The princess and her husband in their
lodge,' Gio countered. 'The mother of the heir

to the throne of Adria in the country that's going to love her.'

'Come on,' Hailey said to Gio seriously, turning in his arms and letting in the cool air. 'You can't really believe that. They'll love the fairy tale wedding. They'll love the baby photos they'll expect us to release. Will they love me when I don't lose the baby weight as fast as they expect? When I want to prioritise our baby's privacy over their desire for access? Will they love me when they're faced with a choice between respecting my privacy and a salacious magazine article about the broken homes and grubby people in my past?'

'None of that is real,' Gio said, tucking a curl behind her ear. 'Those people don't know you.'

'But your mother made it clear that I don't fit in this family and she's right. Don't give me hope or false expectations when we both know the truth. It's not fair to me, Gio. It's cruel. Even my own biological parents didn't love me. They can't have, to have given me up. To have been happy to leave me with strangers. To never try and find me.'

'Do you want to find them?' he asked, and Hailey shook her head.

'No. Not any more. I can't see what good

it would do now. It's too late. Too much damage has been done.'

'Is there anything I can do? I can't change my family. Who I am. But I can speak to my mother and make sure she never says anything like that again.'

Hailey shook her head again. 'No. It's not worth it. I just want to leave it. Honestly, Gio, I've felt like this all my life. One conversation with your mother isn't something worth making a fuss about. But…' She hesitated, worried that this, of all things, was going too far, showing too much of her heart.

'Go on,' Gio encouraged.

'But…thank you. Knowing that you see me—that you see when I'm hurting—that means more to me than you know.' He turned onto his side, drew her close so that they were nose to nose. 'I meant what I said,' he murmured, his voice barely needing to be more than a whisper when they were this close. 'We're a family. The three of us. It might not look like any other family. We might be friends rather than the fairy tale. But we belong together.'

Hailey closed her eyes and let her lips meet his, melting into the kiss as his words hit home. She might not fit in at the grand palace, with the King and Queen and the ballrooms and state functions. But with Gio, wherever they found themselves, for once this felt as if she was living her own life. Claiming the things that *she* wanted.

CHAPTER THIRTEEN

WITH SPACE AND time away from Gio's family, Hailey felt herself starting to relax for the first time since they'd arrived in Adria. With walks around the frozen lake, long evenings in front of the fire and lazy mornings in bed, she and Gio finally had the chance to get to know one another. Sharing stories of their pasts— her struggle to find where she belonged, his to put off his parents' need to control his future. And somewhere in the middle of it, her life had stopped feeling so much like a role that she was playing and more like something that she was choosing for herself.

She couldn't imagine choosing better than Gio. He had been attentive to the point of devoted since they had escaped the palace, and she had to admit that she could get used to the idea of being worshipped, if Gio was the one doing the worshipping.

But their isolation couldn't last because, as

part of their deal with the press to keep the wedding day private, they had agreed to a brief press conference on the steps of the palace. The day before their wedding she awoke in their palace apartment to clear skies and a fresh layer of powdery snow that had fallen in the night.

The engagement pictures had been released on Christmas Day, probably right about when she and Gio had been sneaking off to the ski lodge, provoking further ire from the Queen. The clamour and excitement from both the press and the public had been as ebullient as they'd expected, and she was glad of Gio's foresight in isolating them from it all at the lodge. By the time that they had arrived back last night there was barely any time to feel nervous. The palace press team had assured her that the journalists who would be attending had been warned that questions about her family or history were entirely off-limits for any publication that wanted any sort of relationship with the palace in the future.

She had chosen her outfit with a team of press officers and aides from Gio's office yesterday. Her hair and make-up team were primed yet again to transform her into a princess. All she had to do was plaster on a smile, answer the pre-approved softball questions, and then get a good night's sleep. That last one might be harder than it sounded, she considered, glancing across to where Gio slept beside her. Perhaps she could call on tradition and insist on separate bed chambers tonight if she didn't want to yawn through her own wedding.

She hadn't seen the Queen or the King since Christmas Day and had no expectation of that relationship thawing any time soon. Her relationship with Gio though...warm wasn't the word. They weren't even newlyweds yet, and they had barely seen fresh air or daylight in the last five days. As a princess, she might never be good enough. Never really belong in this new life. But if she made her world small—if she could shrink it down to fit in the confines of their apartment, their bedroom, their bed—then she knew where she belonged. She could feel comfortable there. If it wasn't for the fact that Gio had a country to help run, she would be blockading the doors and insisting that they never leave.

She hummed with pleasure as Gio woke and wrapped his arms around her, and then let her eyes close as the smell and feel and heat of him attacked her. It would be so easy if they could just stay like this, she managed to think before Gio's lips found the spot where her shoulder met her neck and she lost conscious thought altogether.

* * *

She was still grinning when she emerged from the bathroom a couple of hours later to find her hair and make-up team already in her bedroom, making themselves at home at her dressing table.

'I'm sorry, Ms Thomas,' one of them said, 'but we were running out of time and His Royal Highness said we could get set up.'

'No, it's fine,' she said, pulling her robe tighter around her as she shivered. Even if she never left these rooms, the real world would always have a way of finding her. She had no right to a truly private life any more. That was the cost of a life with Gio in it. Make-up artists and hairdressers in her bedroom, and her discomfort with that a constant reminder that she hadn't been born into this life and would never truly belong in it.

Gio emerged from his dressing room as she took a seat at the dressing table and came across to kiss her gently on the lips. Somewhere behind her, a comb started teasing out the knots from the back of her hair.

'Sorry,' Gio said as he pulled away. 'The chamberlain was stressing about the time.'

'It's fine,' she lied, aware that her smile probably looked a little tight. She couldn't say anything—not least because there were staff present. She wasn't so ignorant that she didn't know not to speak about private things in front of them. But later, when they were alone, she would have to. She had to have a safe space. Somewhere she didn't have to *try* all the time.

She smiled as she was transformed into her photo-ready self, and she wondered who had given the instructions for how she should look. She had been so distracted that they were halfway through her make-up and had teased volume into her hair before she realised that they hadn't asked for any direction in what they were doing. So had it been the chamberlain, Gio or his mother who had decided what her hair should look like today?

There wasn't a good answer to that question. Being dressed up like a doll by any of those people was an unpleasant thought. Though she supposed there were different levels of fallout for each if she failed to live up to their expectations.

But there was no time to discuss it because she was being ushered out of her seat at the dressing table and clothes were being pressed into her arms and she was hustled into the bathroom when she insisted that really she *did* mind changing in front of the team, even if they had already seen it all before, as they so delicately put it.

She just had to go along with it today—this might be her engagement, her wedding that they were talking about, but this wasn't her party. Gio, the chamberlain and the Queen had taken it all in hand, and she'd watched it all go on around her, waiting for her cues and looking for her marks. And it made her feel like a child again.

From the time that she'd landed in New York, she'd made her own future. Her art history studies. Her move into floristry. The business and career she had spent her whole adult life building—and which she was about to lose, giving it up for a life of being told where to stand and what to wear and what to say. She had known that accepting Gio's proposal would launch her into a new life. But she hadn't known it would feel so much like her old life. How quickly her brain would fall back into old patterns.

Gio's hand found hers as she stood in front of the grand double doors and gave it a quick comforting squeeze. 'Ready for this?' he asked.

Her well-rehearsed smile didn't falter. 'Of course.'

Smile. Wave. Tell them how much she was in love with Gio. Back indoors. She could do this.

The noise started as soon as the door clicked open, shouted questions and requests to look this way and that. She straightened her back as she walked out to the top of the steps. She smiled to the left and the right. Waved when Gio did and answered the questions the journalists shouted from behind their microphones.

'*How are you finding Adria?*'

'It's very beautiful.'

'*How did you meet?*'

'At a friend's wedding,' Gio answered.

'*What do the royal family think of having a commoner join the family?*'

'*Tell us what it's like going from children's home to a palace?*'

'*Is it true you're only getting married because you're pregnant?*'

'*Why aren't your parents attending the wedding? Do you think they are more angry or heartbroken?*'

Hailey froze. Those hadn't been on the list of approved questions. Someone had obviously got wind of her background and decided to take a chance that she'd answer. And had they worked out the pregnancy for themselves? Her hand dropped to her stomach. Or had she just confirmed it for them?

'That's enough,' Gio snapped, a harshness

in his voice she hadn't heard before. His arm came around her shoulder and he steered her inside, kicked the door closed behind them and forced her to sit on an upholstered bench just inside the door.

She opened her mouth, and realised she didn't know what to say. Because, despite everything the press office had promised her, this had always been inevitable. She was always going to face these kinds of questions, behind her back even if not always to her face. She had *warned* Gio that this would happen, and yet she'd still stood there and stupidly thought that she could be protected from the reality of their situation.

When the journalists had mentioned her parents, she couldn't even be sure which ones they were talking about—her birth parents? Her adoptive parents? She had been an idiot not to tell her adoptive parents, and she felt a sudden pang of guilt. Somehow, she'd managed to convince herself that they wouldn't hear the news. They deserved better than to hear it from this pack.

'I... I...' she started, but couldn't seem to find the next word. She closed her eyes, trying to shut out the clamour from outside.

'Deep breaths,' Gio instructed, kneeling in front of her as she kept her eyes tightly closed, concentrating on drawing in even, measured breaths as the shock started to fade.

She shivered. Somehow, on the steps outside she had been able to ignore the biting cold. But, even though they were indoors now, a draught crept around the doors and her arms wrapped around herself were not enough to keep out the cold.

'Hailey, I'm so sorry,' Gio said. 'I know for a fact that the chamberlain is on the phone yelling at a newspaper editor right now. They'll never get near you again.'

'Do you think it's true?' Hailey asked. 'That my parents are upset I didn't invite them to the wedding?' She focused on that because it seemed simpler than unravelling the fact that she shouldn't even be here in the first place. That she didn't belong and never would.

Gio clasped her hands in his, chafing them between his palms to try and get some heat into them.

'I think you know the answer to that better than I do,' he said. 'But you never once mentioned wanting them here. I think you can trust yourself to know what you want. What you need. What's right for you.'

'I don't even know who they meant,' Hailey confessed. 'My adoptive parents...' She trailed off.

'I can find out, if it will help…' Gio offered.

'No,' she said, her body loosening at last, but her mind still stuck in the hurricane that had started with the journalist's intrusive questions. 'At least not yet. I have to concentrate on getting through—'

She stopped herself, realising too late that those weren't exactly glowing terms with which to speak about their own wedding. Had she thought about it that way before? As something to get through?

The engagement photos.

Dinner with Gio's family.

The press conference.

Anything, really, that wasn't being holed up together had been something to endure, rather than enjoy.

But their wedding? Their marriage? That was meant to be her choice, what she wanted. So why was it feeling like a trap, something she had to 'get through'…?

She pulled her hands away from his with no more conscious thought than that it felt wrong in the moment.

'Hailey?' Gio asked, his eyes still full of concern. 'Is there anything I can do to help?'

She drew herself a little more upright, opening her eyes and bringing herself back to the present moment.

'No. Thank you.' Her voice sounded stiff, forced. But she couldn't seem to soften it. 'I think I just want to go back to our room.'

'Of course, I'll cancel—'

'No,' she said quickly. 'I just need some space. Some time alone,' she told him, wrapping her arms back around herself.

Gio watched as Hailey walked away from him, with the certain sinking feeling that something had just been broken that would be extremely difficult to remedy. He could murder whoever had asked those questions. He hadn't recognised the journalist so they must be new on the beat—well, he hoped it had been worth it, because he would make sure they never worked again.

But that wouldn't fix the situation with Hailey, who had retreated from him ever since they had returned to the palace.

At the ski lodge, where they could pretend they were just a normal couple, she had been open and relaxed with him. But once they'd returned to the palace he'd seen the change. The stiffer line of her spine, the tight pull of her smile. The waver in her voice. As if she wanted to be anywhere but here, with him. The one saving grace of the situation was knowing that they could recapture a little of that isolation by retreating to their apartment and shutting the door behind them.

Now she was locking herself in alone, and he didn't know how to reach her.

They were getting married tomorrow. Right now, he couldn't even be sure that Hailey would turn up. He had a sudden nauseating vision of waiting for her at the altar with a gradual realisation that she wasn't coming.

A stab of pain hit him right in the chest, and he had to raise a hand and use the heel of his palm to force away the feeling, the sudden certain knowledge that if she didn't marry him tomorrow his heart would break. And that could mean only one thing—despite everything he'd told himself, every stern warning he'd given his heart, he had fallen in love with her. He had handed over his heart little by little, so he'd barely noticed that he was doing it. And now it was entirely at her mercy.

He shivered at the thought, not comforted in the least. He'd known all along that the very worst thing that he could do in this situation was fall in love, and yet here he was.

All he could do was trust Hailey when she'd given him her word that she would be there tomorrow. If he couldn't fully believe that, how could he even hope for happiness after that? A year of happiness. A decade.

Would he find himself, twenty years from now, in the same unhappily married state as his parents?

No. He couldn't think like that. He had to trust in the promises that he and Hailey had made to one another. They had agreed that this marriage was going to be based on friendship. A commitment to their child. It was something they had chosen for themselves. Not out of a sense of duty to others, but a commitment to what they wanted their lives to be.

So he gave Hailey the space she had asked him for. Had to trust that she would come back to him. And if she changed her mind? If she decided that she'd made a mistake in coming here, and wanted to be on the first flight back to New York? She would need support. He sat with his fingers hovering over his phone screen, wondering if he was about to overstep the bounds of their relationship. Whether this was as meddlesome as the journalists' questions had been earlier. But there was only one person he was sure that Hailey needed. Who he was sure would jump on a plane in a heartbeat if Hailey asked her.

He picked up the phone and dialled.

CHAPTER FOURTEEN

HAILEY SAT IN front of the mirror, make-up brush in hand, wondering why she couldn't seem to lift it to her face. She had dismissed the hair and make-up crew, not able to stand the thought of them buzzing around her this morning. There was enough turmoil in her mind without additional external influences.

She had been doing her make-up to her liking her whole life. There was no reason why she couldn't paint her face today. She only wanted to look like herself, after all. But she had been sitting here for half an hour now, her robe tied tightly around the ivory silk underwear that had appeared in her dresser that morning, and she hadn't even started.

It wasn't that she didn't want to marry Gio. It was just that, for some reason, she couldn't seem to make her body go through the motions to get herself to the altar.

She thought again about the press conference the day before—she had been pitched back into that unmoored, unrooted time in her life, when she had lingered on the boundaries of the families she'd lived with, and how everyone knew that she didn't really belong. And now here she was, in what should have been the first flush of public and press adoration for a new princess, and already her past was overshadowing her happiness.

She shouldn't be worrying about that today. If anything, she should be worried about the fact that Gio hadn't come to bed last night. Sure, he was probably trying to be a gentleman and respect tradition. He had sent her a beautiful bouquet—no other man had ever dared send her flowers—with a note that somehow managed to be both funny and tender.

But she couldn't help but wish she'd had the already familiar comfort of his arms, the warm press on his lips on her skin to get her through this morning. Her eyes widened at the sound of a gentle knock at the door. Her heart leapt for a second, thinking that it might be Gio, breaking with tradition. But, knowing her luck, it would be her hair and make-up crew, no longer content to leave her to her own devices.

She called for them to come in, lounging

against the back of her chair, resigning herself to losing her peace and privacy. When she glanced in the mirror and saw who was waiting for her in the doorway, a great heaving sob escaped her with such force that she wasn't sure how she'd ever been capable of keeping it in.

'Gracie? What—? How—? *Gio*,' she realised with another sob. 'Oh, I'm going to—'

'Marry him?' Gracie asked with an amused expression.

Hailey laughed. 'If I don't kill him for keeping secrets.' She let out a long breath as Gracie folded her in her arms. 'I'm so, so glad you're here,' Hailey said, gulping for air between words.

'Then why didn't you call me?' Gracie asked, holding her out by the upper arms and giving her a chastising look. 'You had to have known I would come.'

Hailey shook her head. 'It's New Year's. You've been working all through the holidays. I didn't want to pull you away and subject you to jet lag when you should have been catching up on sleep.'

'Pfft. That's bull,' Gracie said, giving her a gentle shake. 'Inconvenience me all you want. You're family. That means I get to put you first, regardless of how tired I am. Gio knew that I should be here. So why didn't you?'

Hailey shook her head. 'It's not that I didn't want you here, Gracie. I did, so badly. I just didn't know how to ask.'

'Of course you didn't,' Gracie said, pulling her into another tight hug. 'Because you never learned that that's what you do with family. That the people who love you will be there for you, regardless of what is going on. That you can ask for help when you need it.'

Hailey looked up at the ceiling and blinked, trying to stop another wave of tears.

Gracie took a step away, folded her arms and looked at her critically. 'Excuse me, miss, but aren't you supposed to be getting married in two hours' time? Don't even try telling me that unbrushed hair and a shiny nose are what passes for bridal fashion in Adria.'

Hailey broke into a smile, for what felt like the first time in days, and Gracie picked up a silver-backed brush from the dressing table and wielded it at her menacingly until she sat back in front of the mirror. Gracie pulled the brush through the rogue waves at the back of her head, bringing out the natural shine that came easily to her dark hair.

'So, are we getting you ready for this wedding? Because, if not, I'm telling you I'd be very tempted to take your place. I don't know where this fairy tale prince of yours suddenly appeared from, but he seems like the real deal.'

'He's certainly very charming,' Hailey said carefully. 'And honourable. I'm lucky that he's prepared to do all this to give our baby the best start.'

Gracie's hand stilled and Hailey couldn't avoid her disbelieving look in the mirror. 'Honourable? Doing the right thing?'

Hailey nodded, aware from her reflection in the mirror that her smile was a little too tight. 'I know what this is, Gracie, and it's not a fairy tale. If Gio hadn't got me pregnant we wouldn't have even seen each other again, never mind anything else.'

Gracie shook her head as she started to brush through Hailey's hair. 'Yes. But that was months ago now. Are you telling me it's been all honour and duty since then?'

'Well, not exactly...'

Gracie cocked an eyebrow, the hint of a smirk around her mouth. 'Meaning?'

'Well...we're going to get married. And obviously we're attracted to each other, otherwise...'

'So you're sleeping with him?'

Hailey nearly strained a muscle in her neck

snapping her head round to look Gracie in the eye. 'Gracie!'

'I'll take that as a yes,' her friend said, laughing, with a very self-satisfied expression on her face. 'So,' Gracie recapped, 'you're sleeping with this gorgeous, honourable man who shares your values and wants the same things for your family as you do. Can you please tell me what the problem is? Because I'm not seeing it.'

'He doesn't love me,' Hailey said simply, because there was no point sugar-coating it. 'So I can't let myself love him, however easy and tempting it might be to fall, because it can only possibly end with me getting hurt.'

Gracie sighed and let her hands rest heavily on her shoulders. 'Are you sure about that?' she asked gently.

'Me loving him or vice versa?'

'Either. Both.'

Hailey turned on the stool until she faced Gracie, and accepted her hug when the older woman squeezed her to her middle.

'We said it was just…friends with benefits,' she admitted to Gracie's well-tailored shirt. 'But I don't know… I think I've been kidding myself that it's not more. But what's the point in deciding I feel that way if he doesn't?

I can't imagine that loving him and not having him love me back would be much fun.'

'I don't think loving each other and never admitting it to yourselves would make for a happy marriage either.'

'You're saying we shouldn't go through with it?'

'I'm saying you should marry him, if it feels right. But don't let that stop you talking. Keep talking. Be honest with each other and see where your marriage could go. Don't decide at the outset it's already everything it could be. Don't make self-fulfilling prophecies because you're scared to be honest with him. And if you can't be honest with him…' she went on, looking at Hailey sternly in the mirror '…if that's something you think can never come—if you want to call things off and come back to New York and raise this baby living with its Aunt Gracie—then I will take you home and keep the world away. It's your choice, honey. You decide what you feel for Gio. What you think your future together might look like and I will support you.'

'You're being too nice,' Hailey said, pushing Gracie away so that she could look up at her. 'I'm whingeing that a prince and the father of my baby wants to marry me. I should be on cloud nine this morning.'

'You deserve someone to care what you want and love you whatever you choose. You have that in me. I'm sorry for all the things that happened in your life that make it hard for you to believe that. But it's true. I love you. And there's no reason that Gio won't love you like that too, if he doesn't already.'

'He doesn't. It's not the same thing.'

'Maybe not. But the fact that you have someone who loves you—me—is. And if that disproves some of the things that you tell yourself are true, then good.'

She used the brush to neaten Hailey's fringe. 'Now, get yourself ready and tell me what you want to do. I'm going to get some coffee and give you some time to think.'

When she was alone Hailey fixed herself with a serious look in the mirror. If she was going to change her mind, she should do it now. She wasn't so cruel that she could leave it till the last minute. She imagined Gio standing in the sunlight-filled morning room, waiting for her, and her heart clenched at the thought of anything hurting him.

'So, we're doing this,' she said, reaching for her foundation and make-up brush. 'I'm doing this,' she said again as she started to apply her make-up.

By the time Gracie came back, bearing coffee and pastries, she was brushing pomade through her eyebrows and pressing her lips together to blot the soft rose lipstick that made her mouth look just bitten, just kissed.

'You're going through with it?' Gracie asked as she took in her made-up face.

'If you know someone who can help me into the dress.'

It was a simple slip of ivory silk with little cap sleeves and a bias-cut skirt that spilt around her legs and moved like water. At the back, a row of silk-covered buttons followed the line of her spine to where the neckline scooped down low, framing her shoulder blades and the pale skin of her shoulders.

She'd chosen it with indifference the day after she'd arrived at the palace, jet-lagged and shell-shocked from the rapid succession of events that had brought her halfway across the world and circling the most exclusive of families, terrified that she was never going to belong.

She smoothed her hands down the silk, where it swelled over her slowly growing baby bump. She wasn't sure about the rest still, but she belonged in this dress. It was more beautiful than anything she'd ever worn. It followed every line of her body, even the ones that were still new and unfamiliar to her.

She looked like a bride. And, she realised, she felt like one as well. Not like someone playing dress-up. Not like someone playing princesses. Not even like someone who was about to walk into someone else's life.

Just her. With her plans. With her reasons for marrying Gio and making the future they wanted together.

'So, are we ready?' Gracie asked.

'We're ready,' Hailey declared, sliding each foot into ivory silk shoes which somehow fitted perfectly without her ever having tried them on before. She had known there must be perks to being royal, but it wasn't until she took her first steps in made-to-measure shoes that she realised just how comfortable life as a princess could be.

An aide stepped into their reception room and she raised her eyebrows in question. 'Excuse me, miss,' she said, her face a little tight. 'There's a slight delay.'

Oh. Her lips made the shape, but no sound escaped.

'What's the problem?' Gracie asked with the characteristic directness of a New Yorker as she came to stand behind her.

'It's…er… We can't quite find His Royal Highness.'

Hailey dropped her bouquet on the table

beside her and Gracie tutted, picking it up and placing it gently in the dry vase it had been sitting in all morning, the stems drying out so they wouldn't drip down the front of her dress.

Gracie's hands settled on her shoulder. 'Stop whatever you're thinking. Right now.'

'He's gone. He's changed his mind,' Hailey said, her voice shaky. She could feel the blood drain from her face, leaving her faint and wobbly.

Gracie steered her into a chair. 'You're overreacting,' she told her sternly. 'This is a goddamn palace. *Literally* a goddamn palace. You could lose someone here because they've found a new bathroom on the fifth floor and have decided to keep the knowledge to themselves. Are you telling me the two of you haven't been sneaking around this place, making out in secret passageways?'

The corner of Hailey's mouth turned up and she felt a little blood return to her cheeks.

'Exactly. He's taken a shortcut or something. He's not leaving you. He hasn't abandoned you.'

'You can't know that. You can't promise that,' Hailey said.

Gracie sighed, coming to sit beside her and taking her hand, realising the extent of her power to reassure. 'You're right. I can't make promises on his behalf. But I can make them on my own. I won't abandon you. Whatever happens, I'll be here with you. You won't be alone.'

Eventually, there was another knock at the door and Gracie went to open it, using her body to shield whoever was on the other side from view. But her hissed whispers weren't effective and Hailey already knew in her gut who it was. It was Gio, of course, here to break things off, unable to go through with marriage to a woman he didn't love. Not willing to sacrifice his future to give her child the security she'd never had in her own life.

'Let him in,' she told Gracie. There was no point in delaying the inevitable. The sooner she could get out of this palace and back to her real life the better. Delaying this wasn't going to change the outcome.

Gracie stood to one side and Gio appeared in the doorway. The perfect fairy tale prince in a dark suit and perfectly white shirt. But his hair gave away his thoughts. It was messy and unkempt, the waves combed through by fingers that never could stay still when he was troubled.

'Hailey,' he said, his voice low and gravelly. 'I think we should talk.'

Hailey let out a resigned sigh. 'I don't think we need to,' she said.

'You don't?'

She shook her head, unable to drag her eyes up from the floor. 'No. I think if we're calling this off, the less we say the better. This was always a crazy idea. I'm sorry that it took me this long to see that clearly.'

She glanced up, only to see that Gio's face had hardened, his eyes and mouth pinching, a deep furrow appearing between his brows.

'You're calling off our wedding—' he ground out the words '—with fifteen minutes to go? Just like that? Are you serious?'

Her eyes widened a fraction—wasn't that what he wanted? Why else would he be here? 'That's what you came here to say, isn't it?' Hailey said. 'What does it matter which of us says the words?'

'You're so sure, are you? And you're okay with that? Sending our guests away and just pretending there isn't an officiant waiting for us in the morning room.'

'I don't have any guests here,' she reminded him.

'I can't believe that is the part of what I just said that you're taking issue with,' Gio snarled.

Hailey threw her hands up, so far out of her

depth that she didn't know which direction to start swimming. 'What do you want me to do?' she asked. 'Weep and beg you to change your mind? What would be the point?'

Gio glared at her, and she shrivelled under his gaze. 'Oh, I don't know, perhaps to fight for this relationship?'

'And that's what you were doing here, was it?' She was angry now, and didn't care who saw it. 'When I had my bouquet in my hand and was on my way to you. If you were really interested in this relationship, we'd be married by now.'

'But we aren't,' Gio said slowly, stalking towards her, 'because I was worried that you were having second thoughts and I needed to make sure that this was really what you wanted.'

'I haven't seen you in twenty-four hours—'

'Because you wanted space!'

She laughed at that. 'And *this* is the time for you to question that? Not last night? Not first thing this morning? When I'm in the dress and am halfway out the door. You choose the very *last* minute to break my heart?'

His eyes snapped up to hers. 'What do you mean, break your heart? You've been very clear all along that you're only doing this for the baby.'

'*I'm* only doing it for the baby? *You're* only doing this so your parents can't force you to marry someone else. I have the great honour of being the least bad option once you'd got me pregnant, so you were stuck with me anyway.'

Gio shook his head, as if he couldn't believe what he was hearing. When he spoke, it was slowly and deliberately. 'I proposed because I liked you, Hailey. Because, baby or not, you were someone I could see myself spending a life with. A marriage of laughing over dinner and sharing our days and, yes, raising our child together in the life that we had chosen. I fell for you—as much as I tried to resist it every bloody day—because of the woman you are. The way you marched into this circus of a family and stared down my mother and—'

She stared at him, trying to process his words, trying to square them with the certainty she'd had just moments ago that he had come here to call off their wedding. 'You've been trying not to fall for me?' she asked, certain that she must have heard him wrong.

'That's what I just said.' Gio's words were careful and measured, and gave away nothing of the emotion behind them.

'And…how did you get on with that?' Hailey asked, still unsure about how to take the swerve this conversation had just taken.

'Without great success,' Gio said. 'Clearly.'

She stared at him, wondering if that meant what she thought it might mean. It was hard to know, when she'd had so little practice with people loving her. The disconnect between his unintelligible declaration and his stern expression wasn't exactly helping.

'So you weren't coming here to break things off with me?' she asked again, still not entirely certain whether this wedding was going ahead.

'I was coming here because I was worried about you,' Gio said, his voice softening now as he took a step towards her. 'Because I care about you.'

'So you still want to marry me?' Hailey said.

Gio pushed his hands through his hair and Hailey's hands itched to smooth it. To take Gio's hands in hers and soothe him. 'Do you *want* me to jilt you?' he asked, his frustration evident again in the growl of his voice.

'No!' Hailey protested, finally taking a step towards him, closing the remainder of the distance between them and catching his hands in hers. She pulled them towards her and held them against her middle, craning her neck to look him in the eye.

'I wasn't trying to put you off,' she said earnestly. 'I thought you wanted out and it was easier to push you away than to admit how much the thought of that hurt me. I still want to marry you,' she said emphatically.

'Erm…not to kill the mood here…' Gracie said behind them, and Hailey jumped—she'd forgotten her friend was there. 'But there's a fairly significant crowd the other side of this door who want to know what the hell is going on. I don't want to rush you, but are we having a wedding here or not?'

Hailey widened her eyes at Gio in question. 'I want to marry you. I'm sorry I freaked out.'

He looked at her for a long, slow minute, a shadow in his eyes that had darkened rather than lifted since he had walked into the room.

'Okay,' he said, with a smile that didn't reach his narrowed eyes. 'Let's get married.'

Gracie handed Hailey her bouquet, and she had to look down at her hand and force herself to relax her knuckles before she crushed the delicate stems. Her other hand gripped Gio's with no such consideration as they walked from their apartment, past an assortment of panic-stricken aides and towards married life.

CHAPTER FIFTEEN

GIO HELD HIS body straight throughout the ceremony, repeating the familiar words of the liturgy and holding onto Hailey's hand as if she might disappear if he didn't. He wasn't convinced that his heart rate had recovered from the horror of Hailey trying to break off their marriage. Even now, in front of the judge, he couldn't be entirely sure that this was really what she wanted.

True enough, she hadn't seemed to want to call things off—but who would want to cancel a wedding with minutes to go? That didn't mean that she wanted the decades of marriage that he had been hoping would follow.

When they were pronounced husband and wife he leaned in and kissed her, the dutiful husband. But her lips felt foreign, as if something had broken between them and marriage vows hadn't been enough to fix it.

Because he had laid it all out in front of her.

His constant struggle to not fall in love with her. His total failure at the task. And she had stood there and listened to him and taken his hands. She had even married him. But she hadn't suggested in even the mildest terms that she shared his feelings. That she might even want to one day. And so, moments before his marriage, his worst fears for the future had come true. He was in love with someone who didn't love him back. In a marriage that he was sure would turn sour one day, and he would one day find himself in a marriage that looked too much like his parents' for comfort.

'Is everything all right?' Hailey asked in the first quiet moment they had, as the photographer adjusted some lighting and they had half a room to themselves. It was the closest thing to privacy they'd had since they had left their apartment.

'Fine,' Gio said, his voice flat.

'Really?' Hailey raised an eyebrow. 'Because you've barely said a word all afternoon.'

'I feel like I've done nothing but talk,' he said, distracted.

'You've barely said a word to *me*,' Hailey clarified.

'There are a lot of people here,' he pointed out.

Despite their decision to go through with

the wedding, the air was far from clear between them. They had left a lot unsaid in their apartment that morning and, once they got started, things could get heated. He wanted privacy for that.

A line appeared between Hailey's eyebrows and he couldn't help but lift a thumb to rub at it. He couldn't bear to see her looking unsure—unsure of him.

Her face turned into his palm, her cheek a perfect fit in his hand, and for the first time since they had been pronounced husband and wife he allowed himself a full, deep breath. This was still right. And easier than talking. This was something they could still rely upon. They couldn't be sure that it would last, but there was no denying it was there between them right now. His love might be unrequited, but in this, at least, he knew that his feelings were returned. This need to be near. To feel skin on skin. To ground themselves with the other's body.

He stroked his thumb over Hailey's cheekbone, feeling the hum of appreciation through his fingertips and the hollow of the centre of his palm. He stroked down further, his thumb finding the corner of her mouth, and then the velvet of her lower lip. His other hand came up in a mirror of the right, and he turned her face up to his, thumb still caught on the jut of her lower lip, fingertips in the short, soft hairs at the nape of her neck.

'We got married,' Hailey said, her voice somewhat dazed as he continued his exploration of her mouth, her jaw, her nape.

'You're my wife,' he replied, feeling a fierce possessiveness in his chest, which apparently didn't care whether she loved him back or not, only that she was his, and close enough to him that he could count each of her eyelashes.

He leaned down and brushed his lips over hers, softer but more sensuous than their first kiss as husband and wife. Softer, that was, until Hailey sighed, wrapped her arms around his waist, leant her body into his and opened her mouth to him.

He kissed his way into her mouth, one hand staying on her jaw, tilting her head so he could kiss her deeper. The other was hard around her back, pulling her up and into him, the hard swell of their baby pressed safe between them. One of Hailey's hands unhooked from his waist and wound around his neck instead, pulling herself higher, and he straightened his body, keeping Hailey pressed against him with one hand on her backside as her toes brushed and then left the ground.

'I can't wait to get you upstairs,' Gio breathed against her mouth when they finally broke apart, and he lowered Hailey carefully to the ground. She looked up at him, wide-eyed, the swell of masculine pride he felt at her blown pupils and flushed cheeks for now soothing his hurt that she hadn't reciprocated his declaration of love earlier.

That didn't seem to matter as much just now. Because, even if she didn't love him back, he was hopelessly lost to her. He couldn't imagine ever wanting anyone else. It was Hailey for him or no one. He had her in his arms, and he wasn't strong enough to let her go, even to save his own heartbreak.

If she was indifferent, then he was the one who stood to get hurt. And he could live with that.

'Your Royal Highnesses?' said the photographer from where he had finished setting up the lights. 'We're ready for you now.'

But he wasn't quite ready to let her go. He looked at her for a moment longer before he was able to drag his gaze away, though he had no intention of his arm leaving her waist. He wanted her by his side, her body pressed against his, for the rest of the day. Just until he could be sure that he hadn't dreamt it all.

That Hailey was his and he was going to be allowed to keep her.

He didn't have to fake a smile for the photographs, as he'd feared he might. He was all too conscious of the stupid grin on his face. And exactly what—who—had put it there.

His heart was on show for the whole kingdom to see, and there was nothing now that he could do to protect it.

By the time they made it back to their room that night, Hailey's head was buzzing in a way that sadly had nothing to do with the large amounts of champagne that had been consumed that afternoon, not a sip of it by her.

No, her brain was a whirling round of wedding vows, Gio's declaration that he loved her, and small talk with an array of foreign dignitaries she could neither name nor distinguish from one another. And she hadn't had a single moment of quiet to process any part of it. The moment with Gio, the kiss, didn't count because she'd been so overwhelmed by sensation that she couldn't think.

She was alone with Gio for the first time. In the silence she could feel the knowledge of what they had done soak into her mind, her body. They were *married*. They had tied their lives together—publicly, lavishly—and it couldn't be undone. Oh, they could separate, of course, but that wasn't the same thing at all. That wouldn't mean they hadn't made promises to one another, in front of both Gio's people and the law.

He was her *husband*—her heart stuttered at even the thought of the word. He was her family. The father of her child. Her legal spouse. And he loved her. At least that was what she thought he'd been trying to say. Except she'd been so dizzy with thinking that she was about to be jilted, and then somehow making Gio think that she was jilting him. The rush of relief that she'd felt when she'd realised that he still wanted her…she'd been flooded with adrenaline and could hardly think, never mind untangle Gio's tortured confession that he'd been trying not to love her, and had failed.

He'd not left her side since that kiss, and throughout the day she'd felt the insistent press of his fingertips at her hip, her waist, on her collarbone, as if he was still worried that she was going to bolt. If she had thought that a wedding ceremony was going to dispel the tension that had boiled over that morning then she would have been sorely disappointed.

By the time they reached their bedchamber that night it was positively combustible. Gio kicked the door closed behind him, and before Hailey knew what was happening she'd been spun around against it, trapped between her husband and the hard wood of the door.

'Hello, wife,' Gio said, his voice barely more intelligible than a growl. Hailey squeaked as he started kissing her neck, her ear, her collarbone. But there was something important that she needed to ask him before this went any further, because she'd spent all day turning it over and over in her mind, asking herself whether she had imagined it.

'Er… Gio?' she asked as his hands went exploring, and she had to talk herself out of letting him do what he liked on their wedding night and having this conversation at a later date.

'Mmm…?' Gio grunted, doing nothing for her resolve, nudging her legs apart, and making her thankful for the generous cut of her skirt, that meant that the silk spilt around their bodies rather than constricting her.

She pulled him closer with a foot around his calf and let her head tip to the side even as she tried to continue the conversation they'd cut short earlier.

'Gio, I need to ask you something important,' she said.

'Ask away,' Gio replied, though not stopping his attentions to her breasts.

'Did you tell me that you loved me, earlier?'

He looked up, a startled expression in his eyes, and with the sudden lack of urgency and attention on his part she cursed herself for not waiting until *after* to ask the question. Because, if she'd read this wrong, she couldn't exactly see them picking up where they had just left off. And she really didn't want to leave what they had been doing unfinished.

Gio looked at her, his breath catching in his throat, for so long that she was convinced that she had made a mistake. Then he started to speak, his voice hesitant, and she felt a thrill of anticipation.

'I...can't believe you have to ask me that.'

Hailey tried to find the ground with her feet, feeling suddenly vulnerable.

'Well, I'm sorry, but things were all rather confusing. And I thought that you might have said something that meant that you did, but I wasn't sure and...now I wish that I had never brought this up. Can you just forget that I said anything and get back to doing what we were doing?'

'I've told you that I love you once today without hearing it back, Hailey. I don't think that I can stand to do it again.'

She looked at him in shock. 'So I was right. You do love me.'

He shook his head, his face a picture of resignation. 'Of *course* I love you,' he groaned, resting his forehead against hers. 'I've probably loved you all along, much as I tried not to. But, really, I know that you don't feel the same way, and there are things that I would much rather do than talk about that right now.'

'What do you mean, you know I don't feel the same way?' Hailey said, her hand coming up to his cheek. '*I* don't know how I feel ninety per cent of the time these days, so I don't know why you get to be all certain.'

'Well, the evidence was quite clear,' Gio replied. 'For example, there was the time I declared myself on our wedding day and you didn't say it back—'

'I didn't know that's what you were saying!' Hailey protested.

'And there was the time after we made love and I asked you what you wanted this to be and you said that you didn't date.'

'I *didn't*. I don't!' Hailey cried. 'That doesn't mean that I wasn't falling in love with you. Just that I didn't know how to stop and I was terrified because I've known all along that you were only doing this because you didn't want to have to be forced into something by your parents.'

'That was weeks ago,' Gio replied. 'And I was in shock. If you think that I haven't been falling in love with you every day since I met you then you haven't been paying attention.'

Hailey pushed him away gently with a hand on his chest, just so that she could get a better look at him, to be sure that he wasn't playing with her. Or had been replaced by an imposter.

'But really,' Gio went on, 'like I said, it's really not enjoyable talking about this when you don't—'

'Of course I bloody love you back!' Hailey declared, realising at last why Gio had been so hesitant to talk about his feelings. 'I left behind my life and my business and my apartment and my friends to move halfway across the world and live under the same roof as your awful, *awful* parents. How could you doubt how I feel about you, you great idiot?'

'Because…you were doing it for the baby?' Gio said, with what sounded like a hint of reluctant hope in his voice. 'I mean, that is what you told me.'

'Only because that's what I was telling my-self,' Hailey said with a groan. 'Because, in case you hadn't noticed, falling in love with someone you think doesn't love you back feels quite inconvenient in the moment.'

'So you love me,' Gio clarified, his hand coming up to cup her chin.

Hailey rolled her eyes as she grabbed him by the shirt and pulled him closer. 'I love you,' she said, looking him hard in the eye. 'I fell in love with you a long time ago, and I don't have any plans to stop loving you for the rest of my life. And you married me this morning so I'm afraid you're stuck with me and you are just going to have to get used to it.'

She was rewarded with one of Gio's life-changing smiles, a smile that could rival a sunrise and compromise the political integrity of entire kingdoms.

'Well, isn't that convenient,' he said with a smirk, 'because I love you too.' And with that he brought his mouth down on hers. 'And I'm never planning on letting you go.'

Later, lying in rumpled sheets and blankets, Gio twisting her wedding ring around her finger, Hailey couldn't help but be aware of the extremely smug grin she was sure that she must be wearing.

'I can't believe we made this so complicated,' she told Gio's chest, where her cheek was pressed comfortably against his warm skin. Gio mumbled his agreement, and she chuckled at the knowledge that she had robbed him of the power of speech.

'We were lying like this three months ago,' she observed, remembering that night together in New York, how comfortable they had been. How right it had felt. How bittersweet the morning after had felt, when she had wanted so much to have more of him but had been too afraid to ask for it. 'We could have just…not stopped,' she observed, wondering how things could have turned out differently if they'd just recognised what they were feeling right from the start.

Gio gave another grunt, let go of her hand and rolled on top of her, his hands brushing her hair out of her face. 'I wouldn't change a thing,' he said, kissing her gently, 'not one thing, if it meant that we ended up somewhere other than here.'

She thought about it as he kissed his way down her body, the utter perfection of sharing a marriage bed with Crown Prince Giovanni of Adria, and found that she couldn't fault his reasoning. In fact, if she didn't know better, she'd say that they'd somehow—blindfolded, directionless and hindered by several key moments of stupidity—stumbled on a fairy tale after all.

* * * * *

Look out for the next story in the
A Wedding in New York trilogy

Reunited Under the Mistletoe
by Susan Meier

Coming soon!

And if you enjoyed this story,
check out these other great reads from
Ellie Darkins

From Best Friend to Fiancée
Snowbound at the Manor
Reunited by the Tycoon's Twins

All available now!